SACRIFICE BEHIND THE FALLS

A VIKING WITCH MYSTERY

CATE MARTIN

Cover design by Shezaad Sudar.

Rune art by BettyStrange at Dreamstime.com.

Ratatoskr Press logo by Aidan Vincent Kise.

ISBN 978-1-958606-17-9

❀ Formatted with Vellum

CHAPTER ONE

ALL THE INHABITANTS of Villmark agreed: this was the warmest and sunniest spring any of them could recall. I had missed out on almost the entire month of April, having spent it far in the north where the weather hadn't been quite so mild.

But I had been in Villmark for weeks now. It was the middle of May, but it felt much closer to Midsummer than that. The sun was only halfway up the sky as I stood outside the council hall, but it was almost too warm on my shoulders. A few puffy clouds skittered across the sky, steering well clear of the sun's path.

The public gardens behind me were filling the air with the smell of growing things. Fallen apple tree blossoms from the orchard covered the cobblestoned road like snow, and the smell as the breeze or some passing feet stirred them up was more apple than flower.

I had a sudden craving for apple butter. Apple butter smeared on my grandmother's waffles.

I hadn't had those waffles in months. I missed being in the same house with her, but she had insisted that Villmark needed me close by. And that she needed to remain in the lonely cabin overlooking the shores of Lake Superior. A nearly two-hour walk separated us. I didn't make that journey as often as I should, I knew.

But she was making it today. Because I had asked her to be there with me when I talked to the council.

I fussed with my new dress yet again. The last time I had been called to stand before the council, I had opted for the traditional garb of Villmarker women: a sheathe-like dress with an over-sized apron and soft leather shoes, all in sedate shades of blue and white.

But my grandmother had insisted the time had come for me to dress the part I played as the village volva. This meant a far fancier dress of alternating sections of red and green with white sleeves so long they touched the ground when I had my hands at my sides. A golden brooch carved like a cat with tiny emerald eyes was pinned to my breast. It had belonged to my grandmother's grandmother, although it gleamed so brightly it wasn't showing a bit of its actual age.

My bronze wand was tucked into a loop in my belt, which also had a golden buckle fashioned to look like a cat.

At least the soft leather shoes were the same. But all together, I felt very out of place standing in the street between the council hall doors and the public gardens. Most of the Villmarkers around me were wearing lightweight leggings and short-sleeved shirts of a simple, almost T-shirt-like design. A few of them were even wearing clothes from the modern world: actual T-shirts with logos on them and faded jeans with sneakers.

Ironic, really, that I would feel like I was the anachronistic one, that I was the one completely out of sync. I was from that modern world, after all. I had grown up there. I hadn't even known Villmark existed until less than a year before.

And yet here I was, standing among the actual descendants of a tribe of Vikings who had fled Old Norway for the shores of Lake Superior far longer ago than even when Leif Erikson had reached Vinland.

But that was thanks to my ancestress, Torfa, who had used powerful magic to save her people. I, as her descendant, was meant to have my own measure of her power.

I wasn't always sure I did.

But the outfit *did* help.

"Greetings, Ingrid!" my grandmother called as she turned the corner from the main north-south road through Villmark and strolled towards me.

She was looking better than I'd seen her in ages, bright color to her now rounder cheeks, a surer gait to her walk. I would swear her long, silver braid was thicker and more lustrous than before.

Maybe it was just the kindness of the sunlight.

Or maybe it was just the side effects of dressing up.

Because she, too, was dressed in bright colors, in her case deep purple and a shade of blue to rival the skies above us. No wand was thrust through her golden belt, but she had added ribbons and long strips of soft fur to her staff.

I blinked. It had never occurred to me that her walking stick was for anything besides walking. But now that I saw it in her hands while she was dressed like a volva of old, I knew full well that it was a magical tool. No wonder she carried it everywhere.

I wondered when I would get one. But I had a wand already that I barely understood the use of.

One thing at a time.

"Ingrid?" my grandmother said, and I realized I had never answered her greeting. "Are you really that worried?"

"About meeting the council? No," I said.

"You still feel that darkness?" my grandmother said to me. Her tone was like a doctor checking a patient for symptoms.

"Yes. All the time," I said with a shudder. The sun might be blazing down hot and bright on the village around us, but my heart felt a cold darkness lingering just out of sight, but waiting to descend on all of us.

"No dreams?"

"No," I said, trying not to sound impatient. We'd had this conversation before. My answers never changed. "And I haven't seen any runes calling to me through my art, although I've been sketching every day. But I know something is looming over all of us. I *know* I'm not imagining it."

My grandmother nodded gravely, but before she could answer, the double doors of the council hall swung open. No one stood there in the doorway, but my grandmother gave me a single reassuring smile, then led the way up the few stone steps and into the shadowy hall interior.

I had been inside before, but the sudden transition from bright sunlight to perpetual darkness was always jarring. As soon as we were inside, the doors were closed behind us. I could hear someone's leather shoes shuffling over the flagstones, but my sun-dazzled eyes couldn't make out even a shadow of a figure.

My grandmother tugged at my elbow, and I followed her down the center of the room towards the raised dais on the far side. Three simple stools—each just three crossed wooden supports tucked into the pockets at the corners of a triangular piece of worn leather—were evenly distributed across that dais, all empty now. Behind the stools were the pillars that told the story of Villmark, dark, rich wood that was densely carved with figures arriving in a ship, harvesting food, meeting the local Ojibwe.

I had not yet gotten a good look at those pillars, although I very much wanted to. But the older pillars, the ones Torfa had brought over with her people from Old Norway, I knew well.

They were in my house just a short walk away.

A single bronze brazier stood in the center of the room, the smell of burning pine sharp in the air as we passed it. The smoke curled up, disappearing beyond the rafters carved with likenesses of snakes and wolves twisting among more abstract knot-work patterns. That wood was old, the pillars almost devoid of their former carvings after being touched by so many hands over the years.

But the thatching that formed the roof was new, just replaced this spring. It still had a green smell to it that mixed with that burning pine smell to tickle my nose.

My grandmother stopped where the flagstones at the base of the dais had been worn down into shallow bowls by the knees of generations of previous supplicants. She shook her head at my offer of help, easing herself down on her knees with only the aid of her staff. Then she settled there, feet tucked beneath her, staff still standing tall. A breeze I didn't quite feel was stirring the ribbons ever so slightly.

I knelt down beside her, smoothing my dress over my thighs then folding my hands on my lap, prepared for however long the council would keep us waiting.

But the curtain behind the dais rustled almost at once, and the three council members came out together. First was Valki, father of the five young men everyone called the Thors. My time away from Villmark, the one that had caused me to miss all the fine spring weather, had been a rescue mission. A successful one; his sons were back among us now. And Valki, who had started to look his age when they were all missing, was recovering nicely now that they were back. Better eating and exercise had bulked up his hard muscle again, and time in the sun rather than sitting by the ancestral fire in its cave under Villmark had brought the color back to his face.

But the black hair he wore tightly pulled back was shot through with more strands of silver than before. That probably wouldn't improve with time.

Behind Valki came Brigida. Her hair had been all silver as long as I'd known her, and she wore it today in her usual elaborate crown braid. I had no idea how long it would be if she wore it down, but that braid wrapped around her head at least three times. She took her customary seat at the middle stool, crossed her legs and folded her beringed hands over her knee.

She didn't quite smile down at me, but her eyes were more friendly than they had been the last time I had knelt before her. Valki wasn't the only one who was looking at me differently now that I had come home with the missing Thors.

I didn't need the outfit to feel it. Everyone in Villmark just saw me as the volva now, my grandmother's successor, despite my unconventionally modern upbringing.

I just had to make sure I earned that respect. I couldn't let these people down. And with my paltry skills with magic, that was an all too likely occurrence.

But the third man to emerge from the gap in the curtains was my best hope at mastering those skills. Haraldr was my mentor in all things my grandmother couldn't teach me about magic. She had the practical skills, no doubt about it. But Haraldr had studied more texts than most people even ever read in a lifetime. He knew more about runes and the old ways than anyone else in Villmark.

Although lately I had gotten the sense that others lurked in the hidden places outside the village, where pockets of other worlds had gotten tangled together. Others who might have more knowledge. But I doubted they could be trusted as teachers, if they were even open to such things.

Haraldr was leaning on his staff even more heavily than my grandmother had on hers. But he, too, waved away any offer of help, preferring to rely on that staff as he slowly eased down onto the stool. The sparse white hairs that hovered halo-like around his sun-damaged old scalp were stirring in the same unfelt breeze that danced through the ribbons on my grandmother's staff.

"We are here at your request, Nora Torfudottir," Brigida said when Haraldr had given her a nod that he was settled. "Is this in regards to the fate of your mead hall?"

"No, I'm afraid not," my grandmother said. "I am doing much better than previously, but I still need more time before I will be ready to take up that responsibility once more."

"Time, and permission from us, both," Brigida said, raising an eyebrow significantly.

"Of course," my grandmother said with a smile.

As if they both didn't know full well that when my grandmother was ready, that hall would be open for business, whatever the council had to say about it.

I missed it desperately. Her mead hall had joined the world of Villmark with the world of the Minnesotan fishing village of Runde. Runde was in the modern world, or as modern as an economically deprived community that existed practically underneath the highway that ran from more important points to the south to other more important points to the north could be.

But I had friends there, and I missed them. I hoped the mead hall would be open again soon. At the very least, having a place close by to get out from under the dark cloud that hovered over Villmark would be a welcome respite.

"What boon do you have to ask of us, then?" Valki asked.

"My granddaughter and our volva, Ingrid Torfudottir, has been sensing a threat to all of us. But the threat is a veiled one," my grandmother said.

"What do you mean, veiled?" Brigida asked.

"I feel it, all the time," I said. "But I can't get a sense of what it is, or what's behind it. I've been meditating on it, and I've been searching my art for runes as clues, but I've seen nothing that clarifies anything."

"You haven't been casting the runes?" Brigida asked with a frown.

"We haven't progressed that far yet," Haraldr said to her. "But I don't think it's needful. Ingrid's ability to use what we've learned so far is impressive."

"Imagine how much more impressive it will be when she learns all she needs to know to do a proper casting," Valki grumbled.

"I assure you, we are not wasting time," Haraldr said.

"I never could make heads or tails of any casting I've tried in my long life," my grandmother said cheerily. "What is keeping the knowledge she seeks from her is not lack of raw ability."

"What is it, then?" Brigida asked, with the air of someone striving to be reasonable.

My grandmother turned to look at me, inviting me to speak.

I took a deep breath. Then I said, "I would like the permission of the council to meditate by the ancestral fire."

"We've never forbidden such from you," Brigida said, then opened both her hands and gestured to me as if offering me something. "Please, feel free."

"There's more," I said, and swallowed. My throat was so dry, it was like the words were sticking there. "I would like permission also to go into the deeper caves."

"Why?" Brigida countered at once.

"I feel like I'll find answers there," I said. What little I had gleaned from my drawing and my meditation on the runes had only shown images of those caves, over and over. I never saw anything useful in them, but I wanted to walk through them myself, just to be sure.

"This is about the darkness you feel hanging over us?" she asked.

I nodded.

"Not to confront Halldis?" she challenged.

Halldis, the woman who had once been something like my grandmother's apprentice in magic, was far from the only prisoner that was kept in the caves under the village. But she was the one who had attacked me, who had so nearly killed me, in my very first days in Villmark. Brigida suspecting her as my motive wasn't entirely unexpected. It wasn't even entirely *unrelated*.

Because the woman, or the being that looked like a woman, who had kidnapped the Thors as well as their mentor Frór and held them in thrall to a pack of Maras, lost in a world of nightmares for months and months, had looked a lot like Halldis. Like they could be sisters.

If they were both even human.

And there had been another woman I had met in the north, a woman named Hulda, who had also looked like she could be their sister. My friend Nilda had gone in search of her, to ascertain what her part in everything was. But all she had found was a long-abandoned village. No sign of witchy women or anyone else. Wherever Hulda had gone, it hadn't been back home like she told us.

And wherever that other woman had gone, if she was a woman at all and not something else entirely, I didn't even want to think.

But I didn't really have that option. Not if I was going to protect my people, which was my sworn duty as a volva.

I swallowed again, desperately wishing I could ask for a glass of water. But better to just get this over with.

"I have no intention of confronting Halldis," I said at last. "But she might be part of this. I'm not sure, and I won't *be* sure until I've tried working my magic closer to the sources of power below us."

"What do you think?" Valki asked my grandmother.

She shifted her weight a little. I was sure her knees were killing her, but the pleasant smile on her face never wavered.

"I think we can trust Ingrid to be sensible of any risks before she takes them," she said.

"If I should find that speaking with Halldis is something I need to do, I'll of course come back here first to clear it with you," I said.

Valki nodded as if he expected no other answer, but his eyes were still fixed on my grandmother.

"Nora, do *you* feel this darkness that Ingrid speaks of?"

My grandmother didn't answer for a very long time. The council hall was so quiet I could hear the soft rustle of her staff ribbons gently rubbing against each other.

But then she smiled brightly again. "I know if she says she feels it, it is there. I *know* it."

The three council members exchanged a series of glances, carrying on an unspoken conversation. My grandmother settled her weight back on her feet, then chanced a quick look my way, her smile wavering for the barest blink of an eye.

I knew she didn't sense what I did. But I also know this show of confidence in my perceptions wasn't entirely what it seemed to the council.

Because I wasn't the only one who sensed something about to happen to Villmark.

But the other person who sensed it too was Loke. Loke, who didn't quite fit in either in Villmark or in Runde. Loke, who had access to magic through means he never explained, not even to me.

He had helped me out of sticky situations more than once. I trusted his actions, if not always his words.

But while my grandmother trusted Loke—well, under some conditions and to a limited extent, she trusted Loke—the council absolutely did not.

Speaking his name now would as good as guarantee their answer to my request would be "no."

But with his name left unspoken, after a few more seconds of silent discussion, all three members of the council turned their attention back to me.

"You have our permission, and our strongest hopes that your quest for knowledge proves successful," Brigida said to me.

"Thank you," I said.

I had expected to feel relief when they granted my request, but instead I just felt a crushing weight of responsibility.

Then I felt my grandmother's hand on my elbow. I was already on my feet, but after so long kneeling on the cold stones, my grandmother needed more than her staff to help her straighten back up again.

Still, that hand on my elbow, it didn't feel like I was aiding it. Not nearly as much as she was aiding me. Her grip was firm, but it was more than that. It was like she was flowing just a little bit of her own magic into me.

She had so little of it to spare these days, but I didn't attempt to push it back into her. Not that I even knew how I would go about doing that.

But even if I could give it back, I knew I was going to need all the power I could muster, and more.

Like the darkness, I could just feel it in my bones.

CHAPTER TWO

I WALKED with my grandmother all the way through town, past the marketplace full of shoppers and past the well in the center of the village commons, until the cobblestoned road ended at the top of the tallest hill. A footpath continued in the same direction, down the far side of the hill to disappear into the forest of trees, all shaking their new spring foliage in the warm breeze. A few wildflowers were peeking up through the grasses that grew over the hilltop, but the overwhelming scent was just the grass itself. It was far too early in the season for butterflies. Alas, it's never too early for mosquitos. But the breeze was keeping them off, if only for the moment.

"I don't like the idea of you being alone all the time," I said when we'd stopped at the point where cobblestoned road became dirt path.

"But I'm not alone," my grandmother said briskly.

"I know Mjolner checks in on you—" I started to say. My six-toed black cat could not only walk through walls, he could cover vast distances in the blink of an eye. As much as I'd never heard him speak, it always felt like I was *about* to. And lately, it felt like what he was about to say was not to worry about my grandmother. He had checked in on her, and she was fine.

But to my surprise, my grandmother was shaking her head at me.

"No. Well, yes, I've seen Mjolner, of course. But what I meant was, Roarr has been staying with me."

"What, all the time?" I asked, surprised.

"Very nearly," she said. "If anyone needs a little quiet contemplation more than me, it's Roarr. Wouldn't you agree?"

I hesitated. I doubted I would ever know how much of what he'd done in those first days I'd spent in Villmark had been willful decisions on his part, and how much had been Halldis using her magic to control him. My grandmother herself had said even Roarr likely didn't know.

He hadn't killed his girlfriend, Lisa, but he had tried to help Halldis cover it up. In Villmark, the coverup was the bigger crime. Even with the possibility that he had been compelled by magic to do so, most of Villmark saw him as guilty. Guilty, but unpunished. Because of my grandmother's judgement as volva.

And yet, in the months that had passed since those days, I had grown to trust him. Yes, he had attacked me at Halldis's behest. And while he hadn't actually killed his girlfriend, Halldis might have gotten away with it with his help, if not for me.

But in the months since, I had seen proof again and again of how badly he wanted to make up for those things. I believed he was sincere, I really did.

But the idea of him being my grandmother's only companion out at that cabin that had already been the location of one murder this spring...

"I trust you know I can handle myself," my grandmother said, as if reading my mind, and I felt my cheeks flush.

"Of course I know that," I said. "I just thought, if you were going to help anyone during your time of quiet contemplation, it would be Loke."

"I wish," my grandmother said wistfully. "But that boy isn't ready for me yet."

"Couldn't you help him control his power without talking about where it came from or what he might've done?" I asked. Not for the first time. Before I had come to town, my grandmother had siphoned off some of his magic on a regular basis, without his knowledge. She had needed it, not having an apprentice volva to assist her after my mother left.

Taking some of his magic had allowed Loke to control his power that turned doorways into portals to other random places. Mostly. But lately, it was often impossible to find him. He could literally be anywhere in a lot of different worlds.

"No. That time is passed," she said. Firmly, because she needed me to know she wasn't going to bend. But also sadly. "He has to be ready to talk first."

"You think he ever will be?" I asked.

"I don't know," she said. "I hope so. He feels what you feel, you said?"

I nodded.

"Maybe he needs to be here in the village too, then," she said. "I suppose you're going to start meditating the minute I leave?"

"I was going to go home and change first," I said, brushing my hands down the full skirt of my dress. "I might have to sketch at some point, and I don't want to get charcoal dust all over this."

"Well, keep your wand with you," she said as she kissed me on my cheek. "And send Mjolner if you need me for anything."

"I will," I promised.

I watched until the last splash of her colorful dress disappeared among the forest canopy of new green leaves. I was just about to turn to head back towards my own house near the village commons when the warmth of the sun was suddenly gone from my shoulders. My shadow that stretched away from me to the west was obscured by a larger, darker shape that towered over me.

But this darkness I had no fear of. I spun around, knowing that the grin on my face was too wide to be anything but ridiculous. But the change in his appearance since his return to Villmark was even more pronounced than his father's.

He seemed taller, although I wasn't sure if that was possible. If the gold tones of his reddish-gold beard and hair seemed to shine more brightly, that was probably just the effects of the sun. But the happy sparkle in his green eyes was definitely real. And definitely good to see.

I hoped it meant the recurring nightmares had stopped plaguing him.

It had been six days since I had seen Thorbjorn last. And it was supposed to be four more before I saw him again.

"Back early?" I asked.

"Yes," he said, but distractedly. His eyes swept over my outfit. "This is new."

"To impress the council," I said, and decided not to resist the temptation to spin. My red and green skirts flared out, then settled back down when I came to a standstill again. "Actually, the dress is new, but the belt and broach are heirlooms."

"I recognize the patterns," he said. His eyes shot me a quick request for permission, and at my nod he stroked one calloused thumb over the cat's head worked into the gold brooch. "It could almost be Mjolner. Especially with those green eyes."

"Mjolner isn't so old as all that," I said. "These have been in the family for generations, and we know for a fact that Mjolner was a kitten when Frór found him."

"We know Mjolner appeared to be a kitten when Frór found him," Thorbjorn corrected me. "So did it work?"

"What? The outfit?"

He nodded.

"I think so. They have decided to allow me into the deeper caves behind the waterfall under Villmark," I said.

"Indeed?" he said, both eyebrows raised. Not quite in alarm, but definitely in surprise.

"Not to see Halldis," I hurried to say. "Just to meditate and explore. I think the answers I need might be down there."

"And you're going there now?" he asked.

"I was going to change first," I said.

"Then I'll walk with you back to your house," he said. "I was on my way to the marketplace when I saw you standing here. I thought I was imagining you at first."

"Really?" I asked as we fell into step together, heading back down the hill into the village. No mean feat, matching each other's paces. His legs were quite a bit longer than mine. Luckily, like my grandmother, I was generally a fast walker.

"I knew it was you," he said, gesturing at my hair. It was a deeper shade of red than his, redder than anyone's I had seen in Villmark. "But in that outfit… I guess it just reminded me of when I would think I saw you, in my nightmares, when I was trapped in that tower in the north."

I nodded, biting at my lip. So far, he hadn't wanted to share with me what he had seen in those nightmares. I had an idea of some of it. I had had to go inside of that nightmare to get him and his brothers out.

I hadn't enjoyed my time there. To say the least.

"Was I like an evil volva, tormenting you or something?" I asked.

"Certainly not!" he said, as if the very idea offended him. "It was just I would see you so far away from me. Like you were just now, on the top of the hill at the edge of the village. Except in those nightmares, no matter what I tried, I couldn't reach you."

"But you did just now," I said.

"I did just now," he agreed. And some of the tension went out of his body. He really had been upset, then.

"So you came back from patrol early to do some shopping?" I asked. We were inside the village proper now, with other people walking all around us. Best to keep the conversation light.

"I was out with Thorge," he said. Thorbjorn was the middle of the five brothers, and Thorge was the brother just a year his junior. The two of them partnered up most of the time, so this wasn't surprising information. "We finished up our sweep early. No sign of anything out there, for good or for ill."

I didn't know quite how to answer this. The Thorbjorn I knew from before he had been tortured by an entire den of maras—the creatures that had manufactured the nightmares that he and his brother had been trapped inside of—would've kept patrolling, as long and as far as he could, to be sure the people of Villmark were safe.

Thorbjorn shot me a look, then huffed out a little laugh. "You think we came back because we're shirking our duties?"

"I didn't say anything!" I said. "Although it would be perfectly understandable—"

"No, it wouldn't," he interrupted me to say. "That's not how I confront things. Running away?"

"Well, then why *are* you back so soon?" I asked.

Then he laughed again, but a merrier sound this time. "Actually, you were right before. I'm back early to go shopping."

"Be serious," I said, giving him a playful punch in the arm.

He was definitely back in full muscular form. That biceps was like a rock. I hid my hand behind me as I shook it out.

"I am being serious," he insisted. "The wedding is planned for midsummer's day, you know. Lots to be done. Thorge wouldn't stop going on about it, and so we circled back early."

"Shouldn't he be the one shopping, then?" I asked.

"His list of things to acquire is longer than mine," he said. "If only by a touch."

"I would offer to help, but—"

"You really want to get to work," he finished for me. "I know. You get that glow, when you're pursuing something like this."

"I glow?" I said. We had reached my front gate, but I was in no hurry to go inside.

"With excitement and… determination," he decided.

"I think that sums up my feelings pretty well," I said. Although inside my own mind, I added a hint of fear of failure and a lot of anxiety about what success would even mean. But I kept that tamped down hard, and gave him my brightest smile.

He just stood there, looking down at me for the longest time. But then I saw anxiety forming lines at the corners of his eyes.

"What is it?" I asked.

"I'm home today, but I'll be gone again tomorrow," he said.

"Of course," I said, not quite hiding my disappointment. But this was how it always was. His job was to protect Villmark from everything Out There. And to protect Villmark from Out There, he had to go Out There. A lot. For long periods of time.

Even if we all missed him and his brothers when they were away.

Even if I missed him.

But he was shaking his head, his face graver than ever. "No, I mean, if you should need me when you're down below, I won't be here to help you."

"Mjolner can find you anywhere," I said with the utmost confidence.

"I don't doubt that," he said. "But I don't know if I could be back in time."

"I won't be alone down there," I told him.

"You're right, of course," he said. But I know my words didn't comfort him. My friends Kara and Nilda Mikkelsen guarded the ancestral fire down in the caves, and they were strong warriors, brave and true.

But they weren't him.

"I know how you feel," I said, stepping closer as a gaggle of loud children went shrieking past us, chasing a pair of squirrels who were carrying a long ribbon from someone's hair between them. Momentarily distracting as that was, it was nothing compared to the way words left me every time I looked too long into Thorbjorn's eyes.

"I know you do," he said.

"It's hard being apart," I said. Then I felt my cheeks flushing, and quickly amended. "I mean, it's hard not knowing if you're in danger, or if I can get to you in time if you *were* in danger. I'm sure it's the same for you."

But the end of that sentence had lifted up on me, becoming a question.

"It is," he assured me, clasping my arm tightly. As if he *still* weren't sure I was real.

"But we always find each other, in the end," I said, with slightly more bravado than I actually felt. "We always rescue each other, in the end."

"We do," he agreed. "But in the meantime, stay safe."

"I will if you will," I said, and he laughed.

I sensed he, too, was pushing a little more bravado into that laugh than he was feeling. But the shrieking kids were back, one of them waving the hair ribbon over his head as if in triumph. Two of the others started to argue, loudly.

Thorbjorn laughed to himself, then shooed the kids away. But by the time they were gone, he was a good way down the street from where I lingered outside my gate. He raised a hand in farewell, then continued on down the street to the marketplace.

And just like that, one of our all too rare stolen moments was gone.

CHAPTER THREE

I WENT through my front gate, latching it behind me before turning my attention to my little garden.

Such as it was. Most of the space was a stone patio, with a small grill tucked into one corner of the walled-off space. There were rows of potted plants, but they weren't looking good. I kept forgetting to ask my grandmother what they were and what I should do to take care of them. Most of what I was familiar with in Minnesotan gardens were things that had to be planted fresh each year like tomatoes. Whatever was struggling to send green shoots up was definitely nothing I had any knowledge of.

But before I had moved in, my grandmother had only rarely used the house herself. It was our old family home in town, but she had always preferred other places, whether it was the lands far to the north where other worlds overlapped with ours, or whether it was in her mead hall in the modern town of Runde.

I doubted anyone had cared for those plants in decades. And yet, I felt like someone ought to.

Then I noticed my front door was standing open. It was a warm enough day for it, and the interior could probably use a fresh spring breeze to whisk away some of the stale winter smell. But I knew for a fact I had closed it behind me when I had left that morning.

"Hello?" I called as I stepped inside. No one had left a coat on any of the hooks by the door, and the only boots under the bench were mine. But not only had the weather been warm for weeks, it hadn't rained for nearly as long.

There still might be someone lurking in my house.

I pulled out my bronze wand. Not that I knew what I'd do with it. But I felt better having it in my hand.

Then I heard Mjolner meow chidingly at me. Like he was chastising me for being a bad host. He came out of the living room to sit in the middle of the corridor and blink at me.

"Did you leave the door open?" I asked him.

"Oh, I fear I did. I'm sorry. I thought that latched," I heard Haraldr say before my eyes—still not adjusted from the light outside—finally picked him out of the shadowier corner of the living room. He was leaning on his staff as he gazed up at the ancestral pillars that were kept there.

"You let yourself in?" I asked. Not quite accusingly. No one let themselves into other people's houses with half the frequency my grandmother did.

But he shook his head, still examining the carvings on the left-most pillar. "No, Mjolner let me in," he said.

"Mjolner," I repeated.

Mjolner meowed. Still chastising me.

"I was just going to change before I headed to the ancestral fire," I said, and started to head for the stairs. But he finally turned away from the pillars to look at me. My eyes were used to the inside light now, and I could see the anxiety on his face, so akin to what had been on Thorbjorn's.

"Can I have a moment first?" he asked as he shuffled over to the closest of my chairs. I followed to sit across from him then watched as he fussed over settling his walking stick across his bony knees then fumbled to take something out of the pocket of his tunic. I was nearly ready to scream with impatience when he finally handed me a small square of paper.

I knew before I took it what I'd see. My next rune. This one looked like an open bracket, like the front half of the letter K without the vertical line to ground it.

"Kaun," he told me as he resumed fidgeting with his walking stick.

"Is this bad?" I asked. He was clearly nervous. I couldn't recall him ever working so hard not to meet my eyes before.

"Bad? No. No rune is *bad*," he said.

"There's clearly something about it that's bothering you," I said, looking down at the shape. It wasn't speaking to me.

Yet.

"I guess it's just the timing that's bothering me," he said. "Kaun, coupled with your request, to meditate by the ancestral fire."

"Why would that bother you?" I asked. "This is the 'k' that finishes the word 'futhark,' right? Isn't that a good thing? Completion?"

"Completion? That's one word for it," he said, bemused. Then he finally looked at me. But he was all academic business now, his emotions firmly back under his control. "It has two meanings, but they are related, even though at first they don't seem to be. The first is like a sore or a boil, of the flesh, you see? And the second is a torch."

"How are those related?" I asked, puzzled.

"Like a torch to light a funeral pyre," he clarified. I shrugged, confused, and he went on. "Our very oldest ancestors used to put the dead inside of funeral mounds, you know. The body would be laid out in the family barrow until the flesh could be separated from the bones. Then the bones would be buried. Later, we burned our dead."

"So, this is a death rune?" I asked with a shiver.

"Death and rebirth, of course," he said. "Or, more exactly, death and sacrifice and then rebirth."

"Like an Odin thing?" I guessed. That god had sacrificed himself for knowledge, more than once, in the stories.

"Very much so," Haraldr agreed. "But it is also a fire rune. But kaun is a controlled fire."

"So spelling out the futhark is the story of the creation of the world, and this is the end?" I asked, not at all certain.

"The end of creation, not of the world," he said. "We started with Fe, if you'll remember, the fire of creation. Now we reach another, different fire. This is the fire used for shaping, specifically of unmaking to make new. I know that's not the sort of art you do, but perhaps you can picture it."

"Sure. But I get it psychologically, too," I said. "Unmaking before you can remake something? When we started working together, we talked a lot about unlearning before I could learn. I get it. But I don't get why it bothers you so much."

"It's related to kaun as a rune of death rituals," he said. "Death rituals are family rituals. It's how we remember and hold close to our ancestors."

"Oh," I said suddenly. "A rune of fires and ancestors? The same day I ask to meditate by the ancestral fire? That is a strange coincidence."

"If you believe in such things," he said with a sniff.

I still did. But now wasn't the time for that discussion. I looked down at the card again. "If I meditate by the fire while holding this rune in my mind—"

"You'd be attempting what I specifically don't want you to attempt," he said firmly.

"And what's that?" I asked. I thought I knew, but I wanted him to say it out loud first.

"You want to speak to your ancestors," he said, as if that were completely obvious.

"And I shouldn't want to do that?" I asked. "I mean, they were volvas, most of them. I have so much left to learn, and they know it all already. Why *wouldn't* I want to speak with them?"

"I know it sounds like a reasonable wish," he said with a sigh. "Perhaps it's not even a foolish one."

"Thanks," I said under my breath.

"But I would strongly advise you against doing so. You are not prepared for what that might entail," he said.

"What do you mean? They're my ancestors, and volvas. Why wouldn't they want to help me?"

"They may have… other priorities," he said with a frustrated sigh.

"Are we getting close to topics you're not allowed to discuss with me?" I asked.

It was just a guess, but the way he wasn't meeting my eyes again told me I had hit right on the main problem.

"Haraldr," I said slowly.

But he interrupted me. "Not all volvas are good people. Not even all those in your family line."

"I should learn more about them," I said.

"You should," he agreed. "But not yet."

"I'm not ready," I said. Now it was me heaving the big sighs.

"I'm sorry, but you really aren't," he said. "Until you are further along, it would be best not to open yourself up to such powerful entities."

I looked down at the card resting on my knee, then traced the shape of the rune with my fingertip. "I might meet some of them, anyway."

"Anything *might* happen," he said. It was nearly a snap of annoyance, like I was trying to find a loophole in his request.

Which I probably was.

"I need you to promise me just one thing," he said.

"What?" I asked.

"Whatever happens, whatever happens *at all*, do not, under any circumstances, attempt to communicate with Torfa," he said.

I gasped out loud. Literally. Not only had that thought never entered my mind, now that he had spoken it out loud, it still sounded like an unthinkable thing.

Was it even possible? To speak to my original ancestress? Across so much time?

But I guess if speaking to any dead ancestor is possible, time itself probably isn't a limiting factor.

But I also had gasped out loud at the grave severity that was in his tone, that was in the tenseness of his body language, and that blazed out of his blue eyes.

He was not kidding around. He absolutely meant this.

"Why?" I asked simply.

I expected him to prevaricate, to hem and haw and talk his way around giving me a straight answer.

But his eyes never wavered from mine.

"You are even less prepared to face her than you are Halldis," he said.

"But we're her descendants. She brought her villagers here to keep them safe, and she worked the protective magics that hold Villmark apart from the rest of the world to keep their children and their children's children safe, down through all time."

"Yes," Haraldr said, but no more.

So I had to press on. "If we're in need now, wouldn't she help us?"

"She was the most powerful volva in the history of humankind. No one doubts this," he said as he planted his walking stick between his feet and hefted himself upright. "She mastered all kinds of magic. Magic from back in Old Norway, certainly, but also magic she found here. And magic she found in… other places."

"When do I get to learn all these stories, Haraldr?" I demanded, but then raised a hand to belay his response. "Never mind. I know. When I'm ready."

"You are about to meditate at our ancestral fire, and no matter what you say, we can all see you are girding yourself for your inevitable next meeting with Halldis," he said.

"I am," I admitted, raising my chin a little bit.

"Think of yourself from just a few months back, when we started this journey of knowledge together. Would that version of you be ready for what you are about to do?"

I didn't even have to think about that. "Absolutely not," I said.

He nodded, a single sharp nod. "Just so. Trust me. I will know when it's time."

"I hate waiting," I admitted as I walked with him back to my still-open door. "I wish I could learn faster. But when I work with the runes, I'm still seeing new aspects of the old ones. It's like, if anything, we're rushing through them too quickly."

"Our pace is correct," he assured me. There was a twinkle in his eye as he said it. "You are still young, Ingrid Torfudottir. If anything, that is your main problem. You are still young, younger than you know."

I didn't *feel* young, but I had a strong feeling that this wasn't an argument I was going to win.

And it would skirt too close to my real fear, that Haraldr, who was already older than I could even guess, would pass on before I had learned everything he had to teach me.

I had seen all the books in his house, and I knew he had read and studied them all. It was impossible that he *wouldn't* die without sharing it all with me.

I only hoped we'd get through enough together before that day came, far, far, in the future. The idea of tackling all those books without his mind to guide me was daunting.

He stepped outside my door and turned his face up towards the warmth of the sun. I had a sudden memory of doing the same myself as a child, when things like the way the sun looks through the red flesh of your own eyelids were still new and exciting.

That was the look on his face exactly. That the sun was still something new and exciting to him.

Then he shuffled out of my garden and I shut my door before heading upstairs to change out of my volva garb.

CHAPTER FOUR

EVERY DAY for the next week I was busy, not just from sunrise to sunset, but during every hour of the day. I would wake long before the sun and head down to the ancestral fire with my sketchbook and my charcoal sticks, then later in the week with my travel easel and over-sized tablets of paper. I would stay there until deep into the night before I'd finally pack up and trudge home again.

But the work wasn't done even then. At home, I would look at all I'd sketched while sitting by the fire and focus on the most significant-feeling images. Only then would I fall into bed, holding those images in my mind in the hopes that my dreams could unlock what my waking mind was failing to unlock.

This isn't a recipe for restful sleep. And it didn't even work.

So I was busy, exhaustingly busy. But it didn't feel productive.

And I had no idea why. What was blocking me? Was the new rune and Haraldr's worries about it putting too much subconscious pressure on me?

The eighth day found me once again by the fire, but I had abandoned my uninspired attempts at drawing. It was dinnertime for most of Villmark, and I had sent Nilda and Kara both up to have a little precious family time with their parents. It didn't take a warrior to guard the ancestral fire, after all. In a lot of ways, I was probably better qualified to protect it than they were.

Not that I said so. All I said was that I could watch over it for them. I would head home myself once they were back. No one was waiting for me there save my cat, and Mjolner was more than capable of looking out for himself. Or finding me, if he was lonely for my company.

I had just picked up one of my thicker, darker charcoal sticks and was sort of hovering with it in my hand, debating between drawing again or packing up for the night, when I heard footsteps approaching.

But they weren't coming from the stairway up to the meadow that overlooked the waterfall, the little river that ran into Lake Superior, and Runde on its shores. That was the path to take to come and go from Villmark.

It also wasn't coming from the deeper caves, to my relief. Despite having gotten permission to go down there, I had yet to explore beyond the few main caverns I knew already. I was waiting for some image in my drawings to prompt me. But there had been none.

No, these footsteps were coming from beyond the boulder that blocked the corridor between the ancestral fire chamber and the larger chamber that opened up behind the waterfall itself.

They were coming from the Runde side, something I hadn't heard since I had started coming down to the fire the week before.

More frightening still, I hadn't heard that boulder move, but the footsteps were suddenly much closer. They were just out of the reach of the firelight.

I tossed the charcoal aside and grabbed my wand. My fingers instantly left dark smudges all over its bronze length, but I could clean it later. I pointed it at the source of the sound, my mouth suddenly so dry I couldn't summon words.

Then Loke strolled into the firelight, hands deep in the pockets of his black pants. His black tunic's sleeves were so long they bunched around his wrists at the tops of the pockets. That, plus its tall collar and the way he was walking with his head down, letting his long dark hair hang over his face, had pretty much made him one with the shadows.

"You can make a doorway through the boulder?" I asked him as I lowered the wand. I still didn't quite understand his powers, save that it had something to do with doors.

Now he just shrugged. "It already is a doorway, basically."

"It's not a *door*," I said. I had seen him use his powers before. They involved opening a door in one location, then stepping through another doorway somewhere else. He couldn't control the where of it all the time.

I hadn't understood why I was always stumbling on him out in the snow, not dressed for the weather. Until I found out that stepping into his bedroom at home could mean a quick trip from the hallway of his warm home in Villmark to some outdoor place anywhere in Villmark, Runde, or beyond.

"There are no hinges or a handle or anything. How can you get through it?" I asked him.

But he just shrugged again. "It's a doorway. That's all I can tell you. And it's a doorway I can walk through all the time. Even now, when the Thors are away and no one else can easily move that stone back to open the way."

"What were you doing in Runde?" I asked.

"It wasn't a planned trip, but as long as I was there I checked in on everybody," he said.

Many Villmarkers, especially the younger people, visited Runde and the modern world regularly. Most never went further than my grandmother's mead hall, when it was open. But a few had made friends on the other side.

But no one had made as many friends as Loke, who had taken the modern name of "Luke" and had spent so much time there most of the locals thought that he was one of them. I had thought so, when I had first come to Runde. Until I had met him again in the middle of Villmark.

"How is everyone?" I asked, and, decision made, started packing up my art supplies.

"Jessica's café is still going strong," he said.

"She was worried about the tourist drop-off at the end of the winter season," I said. There were a few ski resorts around Runde, but their business wrapped up in early April at the latest. The summer season of lake-goers wouldn't really ramp up until June, when the school year was done. A couple of slow months could spell the death of most small businesses.

"Her local traffic isn't just from Runde," he said. "She gets customers from the neighboring towns too. She's still being cautious with her spending, of course, but I think she's doing better than anyone expected. She did say she needs more art from you."

"Right," I said, looking at the stack of drawings I had done during that day.

What Jessica needed were more of my ink illustrations of fantastical scenes from Norse mythology. Ironically, a thing I had been into throughout my time at art school, long before I had known anything about my actual lineage.

But what I had in my hands now was all moody charcoal drawings of overlapping rune shapes and abstract patterns of dark strokes on darker backgrounds. There was still a chance I'd find something that spoke to my particular brand of magic, but even I would hesitate to call them art.

"Probably not those," Loke said with a smirk.

"No, these aren't good for anything," I admitted. But despite my words, I stacked them carefully inside my portfolio bag where they hopefully wouldn't smudge against each other too much.

Somehow, I didn't think acrylic fixative sprays would mix with the ancestral fire beside me too well.

"Not having any luck, then?" he asked me. Then he took one of the drawings from my hand before I could slip it inside the bag. He turned it around and around, as much as admitting the drawing had no up or down to speak of.

"Not really," I said.

"It's darkness, no question about it," he said, handing it back to me. "I'm not sure we're seeing the same darkness, though."

"That's just it, I don't *see* anything," I grumbled. "It's just a feeling. Which, as an artist, I should still be able to convey. And yet, clearly, I am not."

"You're not trying to be an artist though, are you?" he said. "You're trying to touch something that doesn't want your magic all over it. So it's hiding."

"You think so?" I asked.

"Don't you?"

I pondered that for a moment, then sighed. "No, actually. I know when something is hiding from me. It still feels like something. This doesn't feel like that."

"Maybe it's gone," he said. But we both knew he didn't think that was a real possibility.

"I would feel the absence," I said. I was pretty sure that was true, anyway.

"So you're quitting?" he asked, gesturing at my stuffed-full portfolio bag and the easel I was collapsing in my hands.

"Just for the day," I said. "I'll be back in the morning to try again."

"It's not like you to take breaks," he said.

"I'm not taking a break," I said, trying not to get annoyed. He meant well. Even when he was needling me. He was very good at being irritating, even when he didn't mean to be. "I'm just going home to eat something, see my cat, and sleep on what I drew."

"Like… literally?" he asked with the smallest of smirks.

"Not literally," I said. "It's a meditation thing I do when I'm bonding with the runes. I hold them in my mind as I'm drifting off to sleep. What goes on in my dreams after is usually a lot of help."

"But not this time?"

"Not this time," I admitted. I slipped the collapsed easel into its carrying case and stuffed it in my bag with my box of charcoals.

"Maybe you should try the literal thing," he suggested. At first I thought he was kidding, but when I looked up at him, his face was perfectly earnest.

"I don't think sleeping on charcoal drawings is going to accomplish anything besides making a mess of my PJs and bedding," I said.

"No, maybe not," he said, but he was clearly mulling something over in his head.

"Some of my best inspirations have come from when I've fallen asleep at the sketch board," I said slowly.

He raised an eyebrow at me. "I wouldn't exactly call getting sucked deep into a fugue state until you collapse from exhaustion 'falling asleep,' but OK."

I scoffed out a little laugh. "Point taken."

"I don't particularly like seeing you in that fugue state. It's weird and disturbing," he said.

"Is it?" I asked. I'd only experienced them from the inside, of course. Being transported by my own magic was definitely not a comfortable feeling. But it had never occurred to me how it looked to others.

"But it's effective," Loke went on as if I hadn't spoken. "It's very effective."

"I've been trying," I said. "All week, I've been trying to get lost in my drawing. It just hasn't been happening."

"This is the first time you've been here alone, isn't it?" he asked.

"Kara and Nilda are usually here, yes," I admitted. "But I'd hate to point it out, I'm not alone now either. You're here."

His eyes gleamed at me. He didn't say a word, but he didn't need to. We had had conversations about the darkness that comes with magic before. He and I didn't exactly agree on a lot of it, but we had an understanding.

An understanding I couldn't share with anyone else. Because they didn't live it the way Loke and I did.

"You think I'm holding back because they're here?" I asked.

"I don't know," he admitted with another little shrug. "As much as you say you're only packing up for the day, you have a very strong quitting vibe about you right now. And that can't be helpful. So why not try staying here, alone at the fire, for a full day? Or even just start with a night. Tonight. I can bring you some food, if that's your worry."

"There's food here," I said, although I'm sure I sounded distracted as the words just sort of trickled out of me. Mostly, I was thinking that he just might be right. At the very least, it was worth trying.

"You mean the pemican?" he asked, wrinkling his nose. "Isn't that something we only hold on to for the utmost need? I can get you proper food. From Runde, even, if you're having a fast food craving."

"There's other food in that cave just beyond the stairs up to Vill-mark," I said. "They even have military MREs."

"Nasty," Loke said.

"There's also a cot in that room," I said, remembering.

"Better than the stone floor, if only just," Loke agreed. "I'll help you get set up here, then I'll head to the Mikkelsens place and tell them to take the night off. But I'm checking back in the morning. I can slip in without disturbing you."

"Really?" I said skeptically. "I heard your footsteps just now when you were barely past the waterfall."

"You think that wasn't on purpose? I was about to breach our paltry defenses. It's usually a good idea to be obvious about that. The Thors and the Mikkelsens both know when it's me and when it isn't."

I didn't argue with that logic. The two of us passed through the dark cavern beyond the cave of the ancestral fire. The indirect light from the flames behind us barely lit the interior. The starlight filtering down the staircase did even less. But I knew exactly where I was headed, and so did Loke.

If I had been questioning whether this was the best plan or not at all, the minute I stepped into the storage cave, all my doubts were gone.

Two green eyes stared out of the darkness at me. Mjolner was already there, curled up on the cot we were about to carry out to the fire. As if he had known all along that this was where I'd be sleeping that night.

He always seems to know. But he never tells.

CHAPTER FIVE

THAT FIRST WEEK splitting my time between the ancestral fire in the cave and my home up in Villmark had been tiring enough. Never seeing the sun, only the stars and occasionally the moon. Never having time to cook any proper food, only eating what I could munch on while looking over my drawings and trying to get into the dream/vision headspace.

Never feeling like any of it was working out.

But the second week? That week, I never even came out of the cave. Seven nights and seven days, never straying from the flickering flames of the ancestral fire. My life was stone and fire, paper and charcoal. That was it.

I was starting to miss the starlight. I was definitely missing the fresh air.

Also, Loke was right about the MREs.

But he was also right that he could slip in and out without me noticing him. I had to assume that was happening, or else Nilda and Kara would've checked in on me by the eighth night. Well, probably much sooner. If they were staying away, it was because Loke was telling them I was all right.

And he wouldn't say that if he didn't know it was true.

It was always possible that Mjolner was telling him so. Mjolner was usually there in the cave with me, sitting against my thigh as I sat on the stone floor of the cave with my sketchbook on my knees as I drew and drew and drew. But he would disappear from time to time. Mostly for food, I would imagine, but also to check in with my grandmother and with Loke.

I almost wished he wouldn't. It would be a nice break, to see another human face. But clearly Mjolner and Loke both thought I was doing fine without that. I wasn't sure if I agreed.

I felt like I was slowly going mad. All the time alone was driving me insane.

And I had the crazed artwork to prove it.

On the eighth night, I went to bed earlier than usual. Not that time means anything when you're alone and underground, but it was closer to dinnertime than I usually turned in.

But there was a good reason for that. I had run out of paper.

I hadn't planned for that contingency. If Mjolner didn't alert anyone, I would have to emerge from the cave myself in the morning to get more.

But in the meantime, I would just catch a little sleep. Actual, restful sleep. No meditating on images from my sketches, not even any focused work on the kaun rune, which was stubbornly refusing to speak with me. I supposed the two things were related, but was honestly too brain-fried to puzzle it out.

I needed a break. Longer than a single night's sleep, but I would start there.

Or so I had planned. But that wasn't how it turned out.

I know I had curled up on the cot early in the evening. Mjolner had taken his two-thirds of my pillow and lay purring against the back of my neck, always a soothing sound that would send me right to sleep. That night was no exception.

I didn't dream of charcoal or ink. I didn't dream of patterns in the flames or the kaun rune.

No, in my dream, I was just walking. Walking through darkness. Kind of a pointless dream, just taking one step after another inside of a world where I couldn't see anything and I couldn't hear anything save my own slow heartbeat. My hands were sweeping out in front of me, but I wasn't touching anything.

It felt like the perfect metaphor for my experiences over the last few weeks, and a voice in the back of my mind was complimenting my sleeping brain for coming up with the absolutely most literal dream ever.

But then I felt something else. I wasn't walking at random. Something was calling me on.

This was more interesting. I couldn't seem to slow my steps, but I could expand my awareness. I reached out with my magical senses.

The compulsion to follow what was calling me was so strong. But there was something else going on, too.

I could smell something. Even in this dream or vision or whatever was happening to me. I could smell something that was so familiar, and yet I couldn't quite name what it was. Something from my childhood?

I had a sudden burst of memory, a garden path lined with lush, green things that filled the air with their noxiously thick odors. A round hut with a tall thatched roof.

A red round door.

I pulled away in revulsion. The first thing that had been leading me along seemed to reach out for me, to keep me from fleeing. I barely brushed another mind, but it was too late.

I was suddenly, heart-poundingly awake.

Halldis. I had felt Halldis. The strange familiar yet unplaceable smell of her magic, the treacherous coziness of her home and garden. It had been months since I had been in her presence, but I would never forget it. Not after the way she had gotten inside of my mind with her own magic.

I stood for a moment in the darkness, hands opening and closing fists as I slowed my breathing and, hence, my racing heart.

But when it finally sank in that I wasn't sitting up on my cot by the ancestral fire but was standing in impenetrable darkness, and that

Mjolner was nowhere near me, my heart started pounding harder than ever.

It took longer to slow my breathing the second time, but I needed to be calm before I could attempt thinking this through.

I reached out with my senses again. Halldis was no longer there. But I was sure she had been. Admittedly, I had had my share of nightmares about Halldis since our first encounter. But I had also seen her in visions, and the two weren't the same. She had been inside of my dream, not just a part of what my brain dreamed up.

And yet, I had a strong feeling that she hadn't been what had lured me deeper through the caves.

No, it almost felt like she had tried to distract me. Whatever had been luring me deeper, wherever it had been trying to take me, Halldis wanted to prevent me from ever finding out.

I touched the back of my waist, but I had taken off my belt before lying down. My wand was somewhere far above me, useless to me. I checked my pockets, but I had nothing on me. Not even the smallest stub of pencil or fragment of charcoal.

I had nothing to work with.

I laughed under my breath as I realized that normal people would've been looking for something to make light long before they looked for something to make art. Art wouldn't do me much good without light to see it by.

But then my humor faded. It was cold, an icy yet damp cold. I was wearing sweatpants and thick socks, but nothing but a T-shirt on top, and my arms were already a mess of goosebumps. It had been enough, sleeping so close to what was basically a bonfire, especially with a knit blanket wrapped around me. But I must have thrown my blanket aside when I had gotten up from the cot to sleepwalk down here.

I forced my arms to stop hugging me and reached my hands out into the darkness. I took a few faltering steps, then a few more. All I could hear was my own stockinged feet shushing across the floor, nothing else. I could smell damp cave smell, sort of minerally and stale, but it didn't smell stronger or fresher in any direction.

I was starting to doubt I would find the walls of the chamber I was standing in, let alone the way back to the surface.

I've never been claustrophobic, but even still, I admit I was starting to panic a little.

Then a pair of green eyes suddenly appeared before me, and Mjolner gave me an inquisitive meow.

"Mjolner! You found me!" I said and realized as I tried to get the words out that my teeth were chattering pretty hard. "Do you know the way back to the ancestral fire? I mean a way those of us who can't walk through walls can follow."

Mjolner meowed again, then the eyes turned away. The panic was just edging back at the corners of my mind when he meowed again. He had moved a little further away, and I adjusted the direction I was facing and followed.

He meowed again, then again. Every few steps, like a submarine pinging on my radar. He even occasionally looked back at me again, his green eyes like flashlight beams in the darkness.

Slowly, I started making out other details of his body as he walked. His tail was visible, a curl like a question mark that flicked from side to side. Then I could see the features of his face when he looked back at me.

Light was coming from somewhere, but too dim for me to pinpoint a source.

But I was pretty sure I'd find it wherever Mjolner was taking me.

Only we weren't going up. We were going down, a gradual slope but definitely a downwards one. The light grew more orange in hue as it grew stronger. Firelight, but not the ancestral fire. That was still far above us, somewhere.

Then the light started to flicker, casting dancing shadows on the walls of the cave that had closed corridor-close to either side of me. Firelight, no question about it. We were nearly there. It had to be around the next bend.

But Mjolner stopped suddenly, sitting down in the middle of the cave to start washing himself.

I stopped by his side, looking down at him. He was ignoring me. Pointedly.

"Am I supposed to go on alone?" I asked him.

He licked his paw and rubbed at his ears, but said nothing. His green eyes were closed, lost in the ecstasy of his bath.

I decided that meant yes, and crept on towards the bend in the cave.

I really wished I had my wand with me. Or my grandmother.

Or Thorbjorn.

I followed the bend into another cavern, much like the one I had fallen asleep in before. It was almost entirely round, comfy and womb-like somehow despite the cold stone walls and floor. Probably that was the work of the bonfire that sat in the very center of the space, blazing hot and bright, casting flickers of light and shadow over all the walls, making the various stony protrusions dance.

It had always been a wonder to me, how seldom we added logs to the fire behind the waterfall. For a fire of such immense size, it required very little fuel.

But I could tell by the staleness of the air and the undisturbed dust that was coating my socks that no one had been down this way in years. Decades. Maybe even centuries.

And yet the fire still burned.

I reached out a hand towards the flames, not close enough to touch, of course, but enough to feel their heat and watch as the goose-flesh on my arm flattened away.

I could feel magic in that heat. No doubt about it. The fire above had magic to it too, of course. I had meditated and drawn while looking into its flames before, more successfully than my attempts over the last few weeks, for sure.

But this fire felt like magic of a higher level. Older, more powerful magic.

I had an unquestioning certainty that this, in fact, was the original fire that Torfa had brought with her from Old Norway. This was the heart of the magic that protected Villmark and its people from harm. The fire above was just a sibling of this fire, a minor offshoot.

I had so many questions.

But I knew at once those questions were going to have to wait for another day.

Because there, at my very feet, between me and the flames, was a dead body. A woman with long blonde hair just barely still attached to the remains of her scalp. She was wearing a dress in once-bright colors, now faded by time, and I had a sneaking suspicion the fur around her neck was from a cat.

Definitely a volva, but how long ago had she died? I didn't think she was as old as the fire. She didn't look like she'd been lying in this cave since the tenth century, anyway. There was still some flesh on her skeleton, if only a little. And the fine work of the brooch pinned to her dress struck me as more modern than that.

It was hard to see it clearly, though. It looked like she had been kneeling, then slumped forward, her face turned away from the fire. The brooch was mostly in shadow, and I didn't want to disturb the body by trying to touch it. But I was sure it wasn't from the Viking age.

And yet, she hadn't died recently, either. Not unless time moved differently in this place.

Which was an all too likely possibility, I had to concede.

The only thing I knew for sure was that this was not the corpse of someone who had gotten lost in the deeper caves. It might be cold enough in the cavern I had just left behind to die of hypothermia in one's sleep, but she was too close to the flames for that.

She hadn't starved to death or died of thirst, either.

No, this woman, whoever she had been, had clearly been murdered.

I could tell by the way the back of her skull was smashed in. It had definitely been a murder.

CHAPTER SIX

Obviously, my first impression was that this must have been one of my ancestors. All volvas in Villmark descend from Torfa. We're all Torfudottirs.

But I knew so little about all the generations between Torfa and my grandmother. I didn't know their names or their stories. I didn't know who this woman might have been. Or if anyone knew how she died.

Actually, I could make a good guess at that last bit. Whoever had smashed her skull in had known her fate. But no one else. Or else her body would've been taken away from this place. Taken to...

But I had run into the limits of my family knowledge yet again. If we had a barrow or a crypt, or a family graveyard, I had never seen it.

So, so many questions.

I rubbed at my head tiredly. My brain felt thicker than it had before I had attempted to give myself a single night of restful sleep. Yet another task I had failed utterly to achieve.

But it was clear that the first thing I had to do was find my way out of these caves I had sleepwalked into.

Boy, I hoped it was sleepwalking, like normal people did. If I had sleepwalked through walls like Mjolner could do at will, or even through a doorway like Loke did semi-intentionally, I was going to have considerable difficulties getting back now that I was awake.

I left the body untouched by the fire and turned back towards the larger cavern. Mjolner was still sitting there, just as absorbed in washing himself as before.

But something was different. The art bag resting on the cave floor next to him was definitely new.

In both senses of the word, I realized as I picked it up. It hadn't been there when I had passed Mjolner to go into the cave with the fire, but it was also brand-new. The leather handles stood rigidly in a position that had yet to be molded by any hand, and when I zipped it open to look inside, the first thing that caught my eye was the desiccant packet resting on the bottom. Do not eat.

At least the tag had been removed.

Then I reached inside and pulled out a fresh sketchbook, the same brand I preferred but in a virgin state. There was also a metal case of hard and soft pencils, then another of charcoal tools from compressed sticks to fine willows, as yet unbroken.

I gave Mjolner a pointed look. Aside from running out of paper, all of my other supplies had been on their last days, too. The pencils were mere stubs, charcoal broken into uselessly small bits.

"Why do I smell the hand of Loke in all this?" I asked him, peeking in the bag one last time to see a few blending stumps lurking on the bottom, as well as a square of sandpaper and a sharpener for the pencils.

Mjolner meowed, annoyed.

"Well, obviously you told him I needed all this, so thanks," I said. He meowed again, clearly deigning to accept my apology. Then he resumed his bath.

I took the bag with me back into the cave. Now that I had my tools with me, I was no longer so eager to get back up to the world above. Not until I knew what had happened here, anyway.

I stepped around the body to a point further around the fire before sitting down on the stone floor and opening my new sketchbook on my knees. I didn't want to be uncomfortably close to the fire, or too close to the body, but I needed the light to see. And as much as the fire was blazing high in the center of the cave, the corners still had a decided chill to them. But I had a little practice at finding the right spot from my many days in the cave above.

I took out a new pencil, glanced up briefly at the body, then started to draw.

And I was immediately swept up in the flow state. There was nothing but me, what I was looking at, and what I was drawing on the page. Nothing else existed. Not even time.

This. This was what I had been trying to do for two straight weeks without success.

This time it came so easy. I only came out of it enough to be aware I was turning pages or changing pencils. Then the work sucked me back in.

I don't know how long I labored, but when I finally sat back with a blink, feeling the urgent pangs of hunger my stomach had been struggling to get my attention with for some time, I realized I had filled half the sketchbook with drawings.

The first ten or so were the body by the fire, pretty much just as she was now. No sense of how she had looked in life, not even how old she had been or how long she'd been lying here on the stone floor.

But each subsequent drawing had more runes lurking in the patterns of the background. Mostly kaun, but some ase. Odin's rune, never one I had felt a close bond with.

I wasn't sure yet what this was trying to tell me. So I kept turning pages.

The next set of pictures weren't of the fire or the body or anything like that. They seemed to be just generic scenes of Viking life. Not daily life in Villmark above, more like scenes from a book about Vikings. The sort of book I had dozens of back at my house. I used them as references for drawings, more the descriptions in the text than the drawings themselves.

Not the sort of thing I had ever drawn before while in a fugue state. I flipped through them again and again, but they refused to match any of my theories. They didn't tell the story of Villmark.

There were no ships, no view of the lake, no images of the ancestral fire.

They weren't specifically from my textbooks either. I looked them over critically to be sure I wasn't sleep-plagiarizing, but they definitely weren't specifically familiar. Only a general sense that I knew the type of drawing. Stilted postures on figures who always seemed to be talking, with absolutely no sense of what was being discussed.

Then I looked again, a third time.

All the pictures were of men. Two, three or four together in each sketch. The larger groups were where I noticed it first: in each sketch there was one man apart from the others. The others almost seemed to be discussing him, or talking about him behind his back. They had furtive expressions, for sure.

But the one apart, a different man in each sketch, had unfocused eyes. And soft features; almost feminine, although I knew by their dress they were men.

The couple of sketches were there were only two men, the effeminate one again looked like he was trancing out, while the only other man in attendance in these cases seemed to be monologuing or complaining to the sky or something.

I had no idea what any of this was about.

The last dozen or so sketches were darker. Literally; without realizing it, I had switched to charcoal and went heavy on the compressed stick. They weren't exactly abstracts, but I had to unfocus my eyes to look beyond a veil-like surface of charcoal dust and tumbling forms of runes to see the barely-there drawings behind.

They were all of sacrifices. Odin hanging from the World Tree and Odin giving up an eye were the clearest of the sketches. But others brought to mind stories of the sacrifices at Uppsala in the really old tales that were more history than myth. A lot of the darkest patches of charcoal were representations of lakes of blood, flowing everywhere.

The pangs of hunger rolled over into queasiness. I hated when I drew things like this. Like magical forces were using my artistic skills for their own twisted ends.

And yet I had to look over these last drawings more than once.

The rune kaun started popping out at me from every bit of background and even from the veil-like foreground. Just little bracket-shaped patterns in the dust. And yet clearly deliberate.

But kaun was self-sacrifice, and those last drawings really didn't feel like they fit that category. At all. I looked again at the faces of the victims, then looked away. Their horror was plain. Perhaps they had stepped up to the sacrificial stone willingly, but if so, they had changed their minds there at the end.

Was it still a self-sacrifice if you died wishing you could take it back?

I forced myself to look at them all one last time, then put the book away. The sacrifice sketches had women in them as well as men, but none of them felt like they corresponded to the dead woman before me now.

It was possible she had come here, to a sacred place, and knelt before the ancestral fire, and let someone bludgeon her from behind.

But why? What good would that sacrifice have done? And why would the people who took her life just leave her body here? They hadn't even turned her over onto her back, folded her hands on her chest. Draped her in a veil or built a bier of flowers around her. Nothing.

What good was a sacrifice no one appreciated?

No, my gut was still saying murder.

But my magic clearly said otherwise.

I put the rest of my tools away, then brushed the charcoal off my hands on the front of my sweatpants. They were already covered in the stuff, so much so I wasn't even sure an industrial washing machine could get it out again.

I got to my feet and slung the bag over my shoulder, but I paused a moment, standing over the head of the woman I still thought might be an ancestor of mine somehow.

Someone knew what had happened here. And thanks to my growing magical skills, they didn't even have to still be alive for me to get their stories out of them. I just had to retrace their steps, sense the wisps of themselves they had left behind, and let my art do the rest.

I was going to get to the bottom of this. If I had to sit on every grave in Villmark and draw every decaying body's story, I would do it.

It wasn't just about finding justice for this poor woman. Her killer, too, was almost certainly long dead.

No, it was time in general for me to start learning more about the past. About the history of my family.

The darkness may have driven me to the ancestral fire, but now I had so many reasons to keep studying what was illuminated by those flames.

I just hoped there was still enough time to learn it all.

CHAPTER SEVEN

I DON'T KNOW how long I spent walking through total darkness, only Mjolner's echoing meows and occasional bright eyes glancing back to guide me. It felt like hours. The damp cold soaked into me, down to my bones. I started to fear I would never feel warm again.

Then slowly I became aware that I could make out the outline of Mjolner's tail high in the air. It took a long time for the light to build enough for me to even be able to tell that light was coming from further ahead of us.

But then we were standing in the central cavern between the staircase that led up to the meadow and the cave that led to the ancestral fire. The staircase was dimly lit by starlight from above, but I could hear the murmur of voices by the fire. I headed that way first.

The first sensation of warmth from the flames set off a wave of shivering so strong my teeth were literally chattering against each other. I was afraid I would bite my tongue and tried to clench my jaw, but the shaking wouldn't stop.

Then I was fully inside the cavern that housed the fire, and the light was too much. I was blinded, and put a shaking hand over my eyes even as I turned my face away.

"Ingrid!" I heard Nilda call out, but I knew it was Kara that rushed to throw the blanket I had left behind on the cot around my shoulders. She wrapped it tightly around my neck and started chafing my arms vigorously.

"Nilda, she's blue," she hissed to her sister. Then they were both touching me, drawing me closer to the fire. One of them took the bag away, the other put two more blankets around me.

By the time my eyes adjusted to the light, the shivering was back to a manageable level. I was able to grip the warm mug that was thrust into my hands. I sipped at it, expecting some sort of tea or maybe coffee, but it was a thick beef broth. The first savory taste of it on my tongue set off the loud growling of my stomach.

Kara and Nilda were dressed for guard duty, in the leather pants and vests and fur-topped boots that made them look like characters in a Viking video game. Despite the chill of the cave, their arms were bare. But then, they often gave the impression that no sleeves could contain the bulk of their toned biceps.

But little by little I caught details that said their usual guard duty had given way to something more of a state of alarm. The long blonde hair they both generally left loose was tied back in sensible braids. And while their swords were resting against the weapon rack on the wall near the mouth of the cavern, they both had knives thrust in their belts and in the tops of their boots.

"Are we under attack?" I asked.

"Apparently not," Kara said drily. Then, at my look of confusion, she added, "we weren't sure if you were lost or… taken."

"Are you all right?" Nilda demanded.

"I will be," I said, taking another sip of the broth. The warmth from it was slowly spreading out from my stomach, but my fingers had grown so icy they still couldn't feel the heat from the mug as more than a vague sensation.

"Mjolner was with you the whole time?" Kara asked, and Mjolner meowed his own answer to her question. "I told you he was," she said to her sister.

Kara had settled beside me on the cot close to the fire, hands at the ready in case I fumbled with the mug. The shivers weren't yet gone, not entirely. But Nilda stood over us both, her expression nearly thunderous in its severity.

Then she seemed to come to some decision, and her body relaxed. "I'll go get Nora. She's been so worried about you, Ingrid. She's been staying in your house in the village. Kara, watch her while I'm gone. Every minute," she said, going so far as to point a stern finger at her sister.

"I will," Kara promised, and put an arm around me protectively.

"I'm sorry, I worried you both. And apparently mormor, too," I said to Kara after Nilda had left the cavern at a jog. "But it's still nighttime. I'm not sure why he panicked so soon."

"What are you talking about?" Kara asked.

"Loke was checking in on me, right? I assumed that's why you're here now. He noticed I was missing," I said.

"That's all true," Kara said slowly, "but Ingrid, you've been missing for five days."

"Five days?" I gasped. My stomach gave another almost painful rumble. I was definitely hungry enough to have missed so many meals. And yet, there was no way I had been walking around in the caves for so long. It couldn't have been more than a matter of hours since Mjolner had found me in the darkness and taken me to the older ancestral fire.

Where had I been in the meantime? And why didn't I remember it?

"We were debating sending for Thorbjorn," Kara said. "We only decided not to because what could he do that we weren't trying to do already? We searched *everywhere*."

"I was here," I said, although I didn't like how unsure I felt about that answer. "I was lost in the deeper caves, I guess."

"But we searched all of them," Kara insisted. "We had teams tracing every branch, with watchers at the forks so that we wouldn't miss seeing you go by. You weren't down there."

"Did you try looking into the flames?" I asked her.

Kara had some skill at magic, although she had not yet started any sort of training. With my grandmother still living outside the village, and with her own wedding to Thorbjorn's brother Thorge coming up, she hadn't had time yet for lessons.

But even without training, she could see things in the flames of the ancestral fire. Warnings of things happening far away. Sometimes even senses of things yet to pass, although she talked about those even less than the other.

She was staring into the fire even now, but not in a scrying sort of way. "I tried," she admitted at last. "I couldn't see you. It scared me."

"I'm sorry," I said. Now it was me putting my arm around her, hugging her close.

"It wasn't like I was failing to see," she said. "It was like you just weren't here, in this world."

"I'm starting to think you're right," I said.

Then I heard footsteps coming from the cave that led to the space behind the waterfall. Three sets of footsteps this time. The first was definitely Loke. The second, softer tread I guessed to be Nilda. And the third, walking briskly and thumping a staff on the stone floor of the cave with each step, had to be my grandmother.

"Ingrid!" my grandmother called out the minute she saw me. I got to my feet just before she pulled me into her arms.

"I'm so sorry. Kara says it's been days," I said.

She thrust me away from her to search my face. "You didn't perceive it the same way?"

I shook my head.

Loke whistled out a low breath. "Sounds familiar."

"I didn't step through a doorway, though," I said. "I was sleeping here on this cot, and then I was down in a deeper cavern. Alone in the cold and the dark, until Mjolner found me there."

"But we looked," Nilda said.

"Yes, Kara said," I said. "I'm sure it's only been a few hours since I woke up down there. Maybe I wasn't there, physically, until then. If you searched earlier than tonight, you didn't find me because I wasn't there."

"Makes sense," Loke said with a shrug.

"But if you weren't there, where were you?" Nilda pressed.

"I'm not sure. I don't remember anything in between," I said.

But that wasn't true. And my grandmother saw it on my face.

"What images linger in your mind from that time?" she asked.

I suddenly felt weak, like my legs wouldn't hold me up any longer. I sat back down on the cot and picked up the mug, but it was empty. Kara took it from me to refill it from a kettle resting on the cookstone on the other side of the fire. It was too hot to sip right away, so I just looked down at its steaming surface for a moment. The fat from the beef was like an oil slick over the surface, spiraling in a lazy maelstrom.

"Halldis was calling to me," I said. "But I wasn't gone because of anything she did. I can't tell you how I know that, I'm just absolutely sure it's true. Something else lured me away, pulled me out of the cot and I guess maybe the whole physical world."

"And Halldis was just a witness?" Loke asked.

I was still gazing down at my broth. Like I could see things in it the way Kara could with the flames. The pattern was hypnotic. But also, I was very tired.

I took a sip of broth, and the salty taste of it woke my brain up a little.

"She was aware of what was happening," I said. "I think she was trying to stop it. I think she didn't want me to see whatever this other entity was trying to show me."

I took another, deeper swallow of broth. My stomach was quieting down now, and I was feeling more alert. Not remotely ready for a fight, but better than before.

"But she didn't succeed," I said. "I'm pretty sure I *did* find what the thing was trying to guide me to. The thing Halldis didn't want me to find."

"What's that?" Loke said.

But I didn't answer. I just looked at my grandmother. She looked back at me, but all she did was shrug. She didn't know what I was hinting at.

"I think it's a volva thing," I said at last. "Mormor, why don't I tell just you about it, and then you can say if you think I'm right."

"Very well," she said, and motioned for the others to go. Loke looked like he wanted to argue, but one warning glare from my grandmother was enough for him to bite his tongue and slink away with Nilda.

"What about me?" Kara asked nervously.

"You should stay," my grandmother said. She waited by the mouth of the cave, watching as Loke and Nilda headed up towards the meadow. Then she turned back to me with a curt nod.

"I found the ancestral fire. Not this one, obviously. The real one, I think," I said. I was staring at the bottom of the mug now. When had I finished off all the broth?

Kara took it from me to fill it yet again. But my grandmother just stood over me, frowning in thought.

"Did you know there was another fire?" I asked.

"So far as I know, this is the only one," she said. But she didn't sound like she doubted me.

"There is another one, deeper in the cave system. It feels older to me, like it's the original and this is the daughter fire started from its own flames. But we should go down there so you can see for yourself," I said.

"But we searched every cave," Kara said. "Every branching, even the ones that we had to crawl on our bellies to follow."

"I didn't crawl. I walked the whole way," I said.

"With Mjolner," my grandmother pointed out.

"You think he pulled me through walls with him?" I asked. "I didn't feel anything like that. But I was in the cold and the dark for so long, blind and numb. I guess it's possible."

"Could you even find it again?" Kara asked.

"Me? No. But Mjolner can," I said.

"We should call Loke and Nilda back so we can all go down together," Kara said. But then she gestured to the bonfire before us. "This is still something to be guarded, right?"

"I think so," I said, glancing at my grandmother. She gave a very certain nod.

"Even if it's only an offshoot, it's been here for longer than I've been alive. And I promise you, it is a thing of magic, and part of what protects Villmark from the larger world. Absolutely, we must guard it," she said.

"Then I'll go get Nilda and Loke," Kara said, getting to her feet.

"Wait, there's one other thing I should tell you before we go," I said. I found my art bag where Nilda had set it under the cot, then pulled out my sketchbook. I turned to one of the clearer sketches of the body and showed it to both of them.

"Someone was murdered down there," I said as my grandmother took the sketchbook from me to examine it more closely. "I don't know how long ago. But she was definitely a volva."

"But that's not possible," my grandmother said. But, again, she didn't sound like she doubted me. No, it was more like she was doubting everything else she had ever believed to be true.

"Why not?" Kara asked.

"Because I've read the records of every volva in Villmark's history," my grandmother said. "They are my ancestors, so I've read not only the settlement histories but our personal family history as Torfudot-tirs through the ages. None of us has ever been murdered. I know that for a fact."

"Then who could she be?" I wondered.

"Given that you were temporarily removed from this world before you found her, I'd have to say the possibilities are kind of endless on this one," Kara said with a sigh.

I had the sinking feeling she just might be right.

CHAPTER EIGHT

MJOLNER LED the three of us back the way he and I had come, through the cold darkness with nothing but his meows to guide us. We held onto each other's hands and tried to keep our footsteps as shuffling-soft as possible.

If anything, this journey felt longer. But at least I was dressed more warmly than before. My grandmother had arrived dressed for a cooler spring than had been happening when I was still aboveground. Kara had added a sweater and wool cloak to her outfit, then given me Nilda's versions of the same.

And I had put my shoes back on. That helped a lot.

Still, the moment I could detect the barest brightening from the flames of the older ancestral fire, it was like it warmed my very soul. Coming through the endless cold darkness to warmth and comfort was an emotionally moving experience. That probably wasn't the reason the fire was down here, but it was a definite bonus.

As moved as I was, it was my second time basking in the light from these flames. The look of awe on Kara's face as we turned the last bend in the cave and she could see the fire itself for the first time was profound.

But neither of us were as wonder-struck as my grandmother. She let go of our hands to rush forward past Mjolner. For a moment, I was afraid she was going to charge right into that fire as if into the waiting arms of her ancestors. But she pulled up short, and when Kara and I caught up to her, almost uncomfortably close to the heat from the fire, I could see tears in her eyes.

"Mormor?" I asked.

"You were right. This is older. This fire… it's more connected with Torfa than anything I've ever felt before," she said. She hesitantly raised her hands, palms out, as if afraid the fire itself was going to find her unworthy.

"You really didn't know the fire above wasn't the true ancestral fire?" I asked. "Not any hint or clue anywhere about something older?"

"No," she said with certainty. But then she gave me a chagrined look. "I never did the sort of studying you're doing now with Haraldr, you know. I went to the north when I was young and learned from so very many people I met on my journeys. But never in a focused academic way. I've always picked things up by working elbow to elbow with other practitioners. Which is to say, there very well could be hints in the histories. But I've never more than skimmed them."

Kara looked like she was fighting a smile, but warded it off by rubbing at her mouth fiercely with the back of her hand.

But I was astounded. "You think I'm an academic learner? I'm an artist. I'm very much 'learn by doing.' I'm working with Haraldr the way I am because you and the council specifically told me to."

"And you're doing very well at it," my grandmother said, giving my arm a squeeze.

But then she shifted her attention to the body on the floor nearby. She leaned her weight on her staff as she lowered herself to kneel beside it. Then she heaved a very sorrowful sigh.

"Do you know her?" Kara asked.

"I did. At least, I think so," my grandmother said. "Why she's dressed like this, I don't know. But see this pearl necklace?"

"Not something a volva would wear," Kara agreed.

I leaned closer to see for myself, having failed to notice it the first time I was down here. It was a single long strand of pearls, now yellowed with age, and I wouldn't want to place any bets on any of it holding together if I tried to pick it up. The body was crumpled awkwardly, and the necklace was on the dark side of her body. But I guessed if she were standing, that strand of pearls would reach her waist or even longer.

"It looks like something a flapper would wear," I said.

"It was a treasured gift from the world beyond Runde," my grandmother said. "She disappeared in what would have been 1924 or so. But I remember the time well. Her name was Yrsa. She was eighteen or twenty at the time she disappeared. Everyone in Villmark banded together to search for her. We swept the woods and fields, and we searched these caves. But no one ever found her."

"I don't feel like we passed through any sort of wall, but it was so cold and dark," Kara said, hugging herself despite the heat from the fire.

"Something happened," my grandmother said. "I don't know what. I never sensed a transition, and I was watching for one. But there is much none of us know about Mjolner and his powers."

"Is she related to us?" I asked.

"Only very remotely," my grandmother said. "She was not a Torfudottir."

"But was she a volva?" Kara asked. Because my grandmother had specifically told us that a woman could be one without being the other. Like Kara.

"Not so far as I ever knew," my grandmother said.

I chewed at my lip, but there was no longer any way to avoid asking the one thing I had never even hinted at asking since I had known my grandmother.

"Mormor, just how old are you?" I asked her.

"How old do you think I am?" she asked with a mischievous gleam in her eye.

"I would say you look like you're in your seventies," I said. "And given that my mother wasn't quite fifty when she passed, I don't see how you could be much older than eighty, at the very outside ninety. But you said you knew this woman, and that she died in 1924."

"She knew *of* her," Kara said, but she was also giving my grandmother nervous looks, especially when she persisted in just standing there quietly, that mysterious smile on her face.

"You said you remember the time well," I pressed. "The 1920s. How could you be more than a hundred?"

Kara sucked in a breath, then looked studiously down at the floor. I guessed she was checking my math. But she was probably also scanning her own memories of my grandmother. She had known her all her life. I bet she had always looked the same, and Kara had never noticed it before now.

"I spent years in the north, as you know," my grandmother said. "Time flows differently there."

"Okay, but this feels like more than that," I said.

"Think of all you have to master to truly become a volva," she said.

That wasn't hard to do. The image of Haraldr showing me all his books on runecraft and magic sprang instantly to mind. And it brought back the memory of my sinking feeling of panic as I had contemplated all the studying I had yet to do.

"It's going to take years," Kara mumbled.

"Decades," I amended.

"It takes a lifetime," my grandmother said. "I assure you, in my own way, I am still learning. And I'll pass down as much as I can to both of you. But you will go on further."

"But how old are you, exactly?" I asked.

Still, she didn't answer. She just smiled at me a little sadly, then looked down at Yrsa again.

"This isn't an easy trip to make, and I doubt very much that Mjolner will bring just anyone down here," she said. "We will have to contrive a way to bring her back up with us, just us three."

"I can bundle her up in my cloak," Kara said, already taking the large woolen sheet from around her shoulders. "There isn't much left but bones. I don't think she's going to be heavy."

I was enough a woman of the modern world to have an urge to

protest messing with a crime scene in such a way. But we definitely weren't in the modern world. And even if we were, what good was DNA sampling if the suspects had all died so long ago? Even if we could collect anything, what was there to match it to?

Still, it didn't feel right to me. "Mormor, I think this was a murder," I said.

"It's hard to see what else it could be," she said. "She was struck from behind, while on her knees. It's hard to see how such a thing could be accidental, especially in this place."

"Someone lured her here?" I guessed. "If we knew why she was dressed this way, maybe we'd know why she was here."

"The important thing for us now is to bring her back to Villmark," my grandmother said. "She had a younger brother when she disappeared, and another sister born after she disappeared. Or, I guess, died. She has descendants who will wish to see her properly interred in their family barrow."

"Did you see anything about her when you sketched her here?" Kara asked.

"No," I was forced to admit. "There were a lot of images of kaun, the rune of self-sacrifice, and of Odin hanging on the World Tree and things like that. But nothing specific."

Nothing helpful, I added, but only in my own head.

My grandmother was looking at me closely, but the expression on her face was inscrutable. Then she said, "you were looking for a connection to our ancestors. You wanted to meditate at the ancestral fire to find that connection. That's what brought you here, I think. But finding this body, I think it's just a coincidence."

"I'm the last person to say there are no coincidences, that everything happens for a reason," I said slowly. "But it is strange, her turning up when Haraldr was already distressed by the way different events were… well, coinciding."

"She's not our ancestor. She just happened to be by the fire you were searching for. Without even knowing it existed," she stressed.

"So, what are you saying?" I asked.

"I'm saying we'll bring Yrsa back up to the village so she can get the funeral rites she's been waiting for this last century. And her family can rest easy knowing her bones lie with all their kin's. But once that's done, the job that is waiting for you is the one you were doing before you discovered this body. You need to continue your meditations. Or did you feel like you'd achieved what you wanted with that?"

"No, I haven't achieved anything yet," I said with a sigh.

"You said you thought that Halldis was trying to distract you from something," Kara said suddenly. "Maybe this is part of that."

"She was trying to lure me away from the older ancestral fire," I said. "Which I don't think she even knew about. It was more like, she sensed what was guiding me here and just wanted to get between me and whatever that entity was."

"Or," Kara said, holding up a single finger. "She knew this was here, and she *did* lead you here. If there's one thing we all know about you, you're very easy to distract from studying if there's a murder that needs solving."

"I don't think that's what I'm doing," I said grumpily. It wasn't like I went looking for dead bodies. They just kept turning up.

Even really old ones.

"Even if you wanted to solve this murder, it's the very definition of a cold case," my grandmother said. "Whoever lured Yrsa here, under whatever pretext, and wherever they went next, all of that is almost impossible to discover now, a century later. Even for someone with your unique skills. And the culprits are almost certainly dead now. Having the body interred is all we can do."

"But first we have to carry it out of here," Kara said. She had spread her cloak beside the body, which looked positively tiny beside that expanse of green wool. My grandmother and I helped gently shift the skeleton in its long dress from the stone floor to the middle of the cloak. The bones shifted, but the dress held everything together. Even the string on the pearls held fast, to my mild surprise.

Kara wrapped the body up carefully, then tied the ends of her cloak together. Then my grandmother and I helped her get it over her shoulders. It wasn't heavy, but we moved slowly and carefully, not wanting to disturb the body more than we already had.

Then we followed Mjolner back into the cold dark.

And I shivered yet again. If my grandmother was right, and finding this fire was only the beginning of my work to meditate and connect with my ancestors, I was going to be making this unsettling journey a lot.

And I was *not* looking forward to it.

CHAPTER NINE

AFTER A BRIEF AFTERNOON SPENT ABOVEGROUND—WHERE I discovered my grandmother was not, in fact, overdressed because the weather had made a turn to cold and rainy that had persisted so long the sides of the cobblestoned roads of Villmark were constant running streams of water—I was back by the fire behind the waterfall before nightfall.

At least I had fresh supplies with me this time, thanks to the art bag Loke had given Mjolner to deliver to me.

I still had the cot there by the fire, and I still intended to sleep there, at least for the next night. But my grandmother's words were haunting me.

I was going to have to go deeper again. But I wasn't sure I was ready for that.

Not that I didn't feel prepared. I did. I had supplemented Loke's art bag with extra blank sketchbooks and pencils from my house in Villmark. And I had showered and dressed more warmly, in my thickest socks and hiking boots. I had everything I needed, even a flashlight this time.

No, it was more like I was waiting for something. But I wasn't sure what I was waiting for.

But this was a feeling I actually knew well. Back in my art school days, I had on occasion had the same feeling before starting a major project, one that I was particularly driven to do well at. I'd have everything ready, but then I'd find myself simply not starting the actual work.

I've never been the sort of artist who believes in a muse. Inspiration comes through the work, not before the work.

I've also never been a procrastinator. And my classmates who spoke the most about waiting for their muses always felt to me like self-kidding procrastinators. Not that I ever said so out loud. But I thought it. Every time.

But this waiting thing came to me, from time to time. The first few times I felt real panic that I was going to miss a deadline while I failed to get myself going. But then something just clicked, the idea that had been eluding me jumped into the forefront of my brain, and I would start working.

I finally had to accept that as much as I believed inspiration came from working, sometimes the thing I was looking for would hide from me, and I couldn't draw my way into finding it. It would only emerge, unbidden, while I was singing along to the radio while washing the dishes. Or cleaning out my closet. Or some other random task.

So, sitting alone by the fire with Mjolner sleeping on the cot as I sat cross-legged on the floor beside it, I kind of felt like I was waiting for something again. Once I found it—or really, once it found me—I'd be ready to go back down to the older ancestral fire. But until it did, there was really nothing I could do but wait.

Even so, I wasn't idle. I turned over my previous sketches from the ancestral fire, and even did a few new ones as I studied the subtler details of my first drawings. Nothing new was emerging, but I was in sort of a semi-flow, humming to myself as I scratched graphite over the textures of the paper.

Then I heard shuffling footsteps coming down the steps from the meadow above. Someone was coming from Villmark. The steps were slow, hesitant. No one I knew. I set my sketchbook aside and stood to await my visitor.

Technically, I was standing in the space that separated Villmark from Runde. It used to be a space many people passed through regularly, until the council had shut down my grandmother's mead hall. Now, while it wasn't technically off limits, this was the first person I'd had come in that wasn't either a guardian of the fire, my grandmother, or Loke.

The man who appeared in the cave mouth was old, perhaps even older than Haraldr. His body was stooped almost double, although unlike Haraldr he walked without the aid of a stick. I wasn't sure that was wise, from the way he was clinging to the stone wall as he shuffled his feet towards me.

I didn't know everyone in Villmark by name, but after so many months in such a small community, I had thought I had known everyone at least by sight. But this man was new to me.

He squinted at me, and I realized I was standing too close to the bright light from the fire for him to easily look at me.

"Hello?" he called, as if he hadn't even seen the outline of me.

Then some things clicked into place, and I rushed to his side to help him.

He was mostly blind, that was apparent. And he really ought to have some sort of stick or staff; that was why he was so reluctant to move away from the stone wall he was leaning against. That, and the fact that I didn't recognize him, had to mean this was a man who really should be housebound, if not more or less confined to a bed.

"Let me help you," I said, and touched his arm. At first, he grasped my wrist almost painfully tightly, his bony fingers like talons. But then he found my elbow and clung to that a bit less ferociously.

"The floor is uneven, but we can take it slow," I said as I guided him over to the cot. "You can sit down here, if you like. My cat will move."

Mjolner lifted his head and narrowed his eyes at me, but as the old man found the edge of the cot, then lowered himself down to sit, Mjolner reluctantly gave way, curling up on the pillow before going back to sleep.

"I assume you're here looking for me," I said. I couldn't think of any way to ask him why he'd come alone that didn't sound like I was accusing him of sneaking away from his caregivers, so I left that unsaid.

"Ingrid Torfudottir?" he asked. His milky eyes were more or less fixed on me.

"That's me," I said. "What can I do for you?"

"You can bring justice to my family," he said, slamming one bony fist down on his equally bony thigh.

"You are related to Yrsa, I take it?" I asked.

"She was my sister," he said, lifting his chin defiantly.

Now I had to reassess all my impressions of him. As frail as he looked, he was looking very good for someone well over a hundred years old. And not, like my grandmother, a practicing volva.

"I'm sorry for your loss," I said. "I met your niece and her children and grandchildren today. They are tending to your sister's remains."

"I know," he said, his voice suddenly thick. "They are good kids. Good kids. But they aren't going to do what needs doing."

"They've already been to Brigida's and arranged for Yrsa's remains to be interred in your family barrow," I said. "They were quite certain it was really her. There was distinctive jewelry." But such things could be stolen, I supposed. Only I wasn't sure mistaken identity was what had this man so upset just now. Upset enough to walk out of town and down into the caves to find me. Me, not Brigida, who dealt with all the funerary needs in Villmark.

"Yes, the pearls. I don't doubt it was her," he said.

"I'm sorry… what did you say your name was?" I asked.

"Vali," he said, thumping a hand on his own chest.

"Vali. I'm sorry, Vali, but I don't quite understand what you want from me?"

"I need you to find out who did this to my sister," he said, as if it were the most obvious thing in the world.

"I'm not sure that's even possible," I said. "It was so long ago."

"Isn't that what you do? Solve murders?" he asked, like he was leveling a challenge at me.

"I'm a volva," I said.

"Nora is the volva," he said shortly. "You solve murders."

"Fair enough," I said, not really wanting to argue about my job description. "But I don't know if I can solve this one. And even if I did, it's very unlikely I'll find the culprit still alive."

"Of course not," he said. "I was ten at the time. Whoever killed her would be older even than me. No one here is older than me."

I was going to argue that point. Surely my grandmother was older, and he must know that.

Only what if he didn't? Kara didn't seem to know any better than I did just how old she was.

Clearly, there was something at least magic-adjacent going on with all that. Something that made people not question or even really think about her age.

But it wasn't really relevant to what Vali was trying to ask me to do.

"What justice can I find for your sister?" I asked him. "Do you just want a name? That's all?"

"That's all?" he repeated in an almost mocking tone. "That's plenty!"

"I don't follow you," I admitted.

He blew out a frustrated breath, mumbling something to himself about young people today and the loss of the old ways. Then he sort of fixed those milky eyes on me again and said, "a name is all I need. Whoever murdered my sister got away with it and lived a long and for all I know happy life, free of repercussions. But a blood price is still owed. I have descendants, or rather my sister has. What was done to Yrsa that was left unanswered still haunts them. I can see it."

"You think they're haunted?" I said. I knew he didn't mean that literally. This wasn't a ghost lurking in their houses, shaking chains. But I had met what I had thought was the whole family that afternoon at Brigida's house when they had come to receive the body. They had been subdued, but not particularly mournful.

Which made sense. They had never even really known her, she had died so long ago. Her younger sister, the one they all descended from, was also dead for more than a decade. They may have heard stories about Yrsa, but they hadn't had a personal connection with her, any of them.

They had been anything but haunted. None of them had demanded to know what happened, beyond what my grandmother had explained to them. It was clear to all of them this was a tragedy from the past that would likely remain a mystery. But they had her bones back, and that was good enough.

Except, for Vali, it clearly wasn't.

"They didn't seem haunted when I met them," I said. "But I admit I left before they were done speaking with my grandmother. Did you speak with her? Nora, I mean?"

Grief counseling was definitely more her area than mine. Which was why I had hustled back down to be alone in a cave.

But Vali just snorted at me. "How many times do I have to explain? What I need is a murder solved, and that's your job."

"I don't think I can do this for you," I told him. "I could try. I have magic that can sometimes tell me what happened. I tried it once and didn't get any answers, but I suppose I could always look again. But I can't promise it will even work. And, to be honest, I still don't understand what I can give you besides the closure of having your sister's remains back in your family's care."

"I need the name," he insisted. "I need the name of the murder. Because whoever it was, their family owes mine a blood price."

I didn't say what I thought about that. Because the idea that it was terribly unfair to punish the children or even the grandchildren of a murderer was still very foreign to the people of Villmark. Even the ones who visited the modern world from time to time. This old man wasn't going to want to hear my views on that at all.

But he wasn't waiting for a response from me. He pushed himself up off the cot, brushing away my hands when I attempted to help him. He started to leave the cave. If it's possible to aggressively shuffle away, that was what he was doing.

But he turned before leaving the cave entirely to look in my general direction and raise a bony finger at me. "I need that name for the blood price owed. It will be paid. But I also need it to fix my curse onto. I've been weaving this curse throughout my life. I've refused to die with that curse still untethered. But you give me that name, and I can finally send that curse on its way and die in peace."

"Is this curse aimed at just the actual murderer, or the murderer's whole family?" I asked.

But he just scoffed and shuffled away.

Which was answer enough. But I didn't like it.

CHAPTER TEN

THERE WAS no staying alone in the cave after that. And I certainly wasn't going to go back to the scene of the crime. Not when it felt like solving the murder would actually be a *bad* thing this time.

Instead, I did the one thing I never thought I'd do without being summoned.

I went to see the council.

This wasn't as simple as just going to the hall. I was sure, at this late evening hour closer to bedtime than dinnertime, no one would be there. But I sent Mjolner with messages to fetch Haraldr and Valki while I went to Brigida's house myself.

"Ingrid Torfudottir," she said to me blandly when she had opened her door.

"Oh, good! I didn't wake you," I said. She was still dressed as she had been that afternoon, her hair still in its elaborate crown braid, her fingers still glittering with rings.

She raised an eyebrow at me, and I realized what I should've said was more an apology for disturbing her so late in the day. But she just told me, "Your grandmother has gone back to the lake, and the bereaved family has taken the remains and left. They were entirely satisfied with what answers your grandmother could give them."

"Not the whole family," I said. The eyebrow arched further at this statement. "I would like to confer with the council," I said, and she gave a tiny laugh, shaking her head. "I know it's late—" I started to say.

"No, it's not a problem," she said. "It just isn't something I thought I'd ever hear you say."

"I don't know what to do," I admitted.

"Something else has happened," she guessed.

I nodded glumly.

"I'll summon the others," she said, but I caught her arm before she could move away from the door.

"I've already asked them to meet us at the hall. If that's all right," I said.

"Let me grab my cloak," she said. She snatched it from a hook just out of my line of sight, then stepped outside before swinging it around her shoulders, already following me down the walk towards the gate to the street.

"How late was it when my grandmother left?" I asked.

"After dark," Brigida said. "Does that worry you? Or were you hoping to call her back?"

I *was* worried. But if there was a way to convince my independent-minded grandmother not to traipse through the forest on a two-hour hike on her own after dark, I didn't know it. And the supercilious look Brigida was giving me told me she knew it. The idea that I might even try was amusing her, apparently.

"I don't think I need her back," I said. "Not yet, anyway."

"Your taking a lot of her responsibilities on your shoulders these days," she said, a little too casually.

"The most important thing I can do right now is whatever helps my grandmother recover from overusing her magic," I said.

"Agreed," she said, but I knew she knew what I was going to say next.

I said it anyway. "So she can open the mead hall again."

To my surprise, she didn't argue with me. She just heaved a sigh and then let it go.

We had reached the doors of the council hall anyway, and when she swung them open, I saw light coming from further within. Valki and Haraldr both were already there.

"We'll go to the back room, I think," Brigida said as she took off her cloak.

I didn't know quite what she meant, but Valki and Haraldr both nodded, then disappeared through the curtain at the back of the dais. Brigida climbed the steps to follow, but I hesitated.

Was I supposed to go back there? It felt wrong. Every time my grandmother had been here, she had been kneeling on the floor where I stood now. Wasn't I supposed to do that too?

"Ingrid?"

"Do you want me to wait here?" I asked, shifting until I was standing in the spot I usually knelt on.

"What possible good would that do?" she asked, and motioned impatiently for me to follow her through the curtain.

I don't know what I expected to find on the other side of that curtain. The only image my mind could conjure was scenes from movies, of a sacristy in a Catholic church.

I was pretty sure this wouldn't be that. But I had no idea what the pagan Viking equivalent would be.

Then I was pushing my way through the curtains and saw I was in a cozy little kitchen like in any of the homes down in Runde. The appliances were old, but not as old as the building they were standing in. The stove where Haraldr was putting a kettle on to boil was a particularly hideous shade of harvest gold, and he bent to light the gas with a match to get the flame going.

The refrigerator beside it was avocado green, and Valki had to pull the handle with a jerk to unlatch the door. The light inside flickered so badly it actually sputtered dark, then light again several times as he took a wheel of soft cheese out of the crisper drawer. He set this on a cutting board next to a plate where Brigida was arranging slices of crispbread.

"We don't do late meetings without snacks," Valki told me in a low tone, like he was reciting from a holy book.

"Of course," I said, still hovering uncertainly just inside the curtains. There were four chairs around the formica table, the sort of all-metal chairs that one usually sees on a navy ship.

None of it fit stylistically under the thatched roof and heavy timbers covered in Norse patterns that hung low overhead.

And yet, in another way, it kind of did.

"This is familiar," I said, waggling my fingers at all of it. The yellow linoleum underfoot, the faded formica of the countertops, the little vine border that traced around the tabletop in a repeating pattern. "This is like the mead hall down in Runde when it's not a mead hall. When it's just a meeting hall for the local community."

"Our predecessors installed all this," Valki said as he took a second wheel of cheese out of the refrigerator, then opened a drawer to fetch a slicer. The kind that cuts soft cheese with a span of wire.

"Please sit, eat with us, and tell us what's on your mind," Haraldr said, gesturing for me to take the chair closest to me. I slid into it, but my brain was still too boggled by the sight of the kitchen to even remember why I was there.

"Our problem with the mead hall was never the modern appliances there," Brigida said as she sat beside me. "And we have no problem with modern appliances in Villmark either. It's the casual mixing of the two worlds that is a problem."

"Without your grandmother's magic working at its finest to protect us from being perceived by other forces, it isn't safe," Haraldr said as he brought a tray of tea mugs to the table and shared them out.

Valki handed me a plate of crispbread topped with cheese and dollops of strawberry jam. "It certainly seems as if the growing threat to Villmark is from within the protective sphere that Torfa cast over us so many years before. But that could be a ruse. A misdirect to draw our attention away from the real threat."

'When her magic is back, she will want to open the hall again," I said. I didn't need to tell them she wouldn't take "no" for an answer. They knew that better than I did.

"When her magic is back, we'll discuss it," Brigida said. "But there was something else you wanted to discuss now."

Haraldr poured boiling water into each of the mugs, and the sweet smell of mint and the Christmas tree smell of juniper berries were suddenly thick in the air. Brigida took a bite of crispbread and cheese but looked at me expectantly as she chewed.

I swallowed hard, then told them all everything that had happened with Vali in the cave.

When I was finished, they all three were deep in thought. But I was hungry myself. I reached for one of the crispbreads on my plate and crunched into it, leaning over the plate just in time as a cascade of crumbs fell away from the cheese.

Brigida had made it look so elegant when she had eaten hers.

"I confess, I didn't know that Vali still lived," Valki said at last.

"I did," Haraldr said. "But he doesn't see visitors. Not this last dozen years or more. He lives with his sister's oldest daughter, but I don't imagine even she sees much of him. He's always been a recluse. Or, at least, as long as I've known him."

"The family at my house today never mentioned him once," Brigida said. But then she frowned. "Although thinking back, that might have been deliberate. Nora had a look to her, like she knew there was something they weren't saying. But she gets that look a lot."

The other two chuckled and nodded, but only briefly.

"He wants me to find out who killed his sister," I said, trying to bring them back to the main point.

"If that is something you can find out, it would be good for all of us to know," Valki said. "If a blood price is owed, it must be paid."

"Why?" I asked.

Valki just stared at me like I'd asked why plants needed sunlight to grow or something.

But Haraldr took a sip of his tea, then said, "You remember when I taught you about hamingja?"

"The karma that descends through families?" I said. "It was tied to luck and happiness, right?"

"Luck and happiness when your hamingja is good," Haraldr said. "But a family that owes a blood price that it didn't pay? That's bad. And until it is paid, no family can expect much luck or happiness."

"So finding out who did this, even though the actual murderer is likely long since dead, is still a boon to the community," Valki said.

"That's all well and good," I said. "I'm all about giving people closure as well as justice. But Vali said he would curse the family. Can he do that?"

"Legally? Of course," Brigida said.

"Seriously?" I said. I just couldn't wrap my mind around it. "If the actual perpetrator is dead, and the family has paid this blood price, why do we need a curse?"

"No one *needs* a curse," Valki said.

"Vali feels like he does," I said.

"The question remains whether he can actually do it," Haraldr said, tapping his lip with his steepled fingers. "It doesn't take a volva to curse someone. But it does take something. Some skill of his own, some artifact that's fallen into his possession."

"Artifacts," Valki growled. "My sons are never with me by my home fire because of these artifacts that keep 'falling' into the wrong hands."

"So that might have happened again?" I asked.

"Well, you said he told you that he's been working on this curse his entire lifetime, right?" Haraldr said. "The artifacts are more a recent problem."

"We assume," Valki said.

"So it's possible when I find out who murdered Yrsa, Vali can do his curse, but nothing else will happen?" I asked.

"It's possible," Haraldr said evenly.

"That's a secondary matter," Yrsa said. "Primary is the matter of the blood price owed. Ingrid, if you can, you should find out who did this thing. For the good of all Villmark."

"And if I get the name of the culprit?" I asked.

They all exchanged silent glances and knowing nods. Then Brigida spoke again.

"If you get the name, you will bring it to us first. We will decide who else needs to know."

"And if I don't get a name?" I asked.

"It would be better if you could," she said, and gave my hand an encouraging squeeze.

I said my goodbyes, then headed back out into the night, but my head was in a daze.

What had I just agreed to? To solve a case that had gone nearly a century cold?

It sounded impossible, but it wasn't like I didn't know where to start.

I had to go back down to the deeper fire. Again.

But I still didn't feel ready. What if I never did?

CHAPTER ELEVEN

I WENT BACK UNDERGROUND, determined to go at once back to the older ancestral fire. It felt like the thing I had been waiting for had happened. As usual, it had been about the last thing I had expected: Vali and his curse. But then again, if I had expected it, I wouldn't have had to wait to see what it was before I could use it for inspiration.

But this was a weird sort of inspiration. Despite the council's assurances they would deal with things, I was not at all eager to be party to cursing anyone because of something someone they were related to had done a century before.

But I did want to know what had happened to Yrsa.

Only, as eager as I was, when I got back to the fire behind the waterfall, Mjolner wasn't there. And he didn't come when I called him.

It felt deliberate. Like he didn't approve.

After several minutes, I had to accept he wasn't going to help me get back down to the other fire. So I slung my art bag over my shoulder, picked up my flashlight, and headed down into the dark on my own.

After hours and hours of stumbling around down one blind passage after another, I had to admit that wherever Mjolner had taken me before, I couldn't go that way again without him. I made my way back to the main cavern to see the midday sun streaming down the staircase that led up to the meadow.

And Haraldr waiting for me by the ancestral fire.

"No luck?" he said as I dragged my feet into the room. I was very, very tired.

"No," I said, dropping my bag to the stone floor. Then I narrowed my eyes at him. "How did you know?"

"Well," Haraldr said, lifting his hand, and I saw Mjolner there, curled up completely content on his lap.

"I can't find the other fire without him," I said.

"Yes, I thought as much," Haraldr said with the faintest hint of a grin. "Perhaps he's trying to tell you something?"

"That I shouldn't solve this case?" I said with a sigh.

"Oh, I don't think it's that at all," he said, then gently moved Mjolner off his lap so he could stand up. "I think it's just that you're not ready to go back there yet. Or, at least, that's not where you should start."

"You think I should start with the settlement records?" I said. I tried not to sound too eager. But I've never wanted to focus on book research more.

"I've already pulled the appropriate volumes. I can sum them up for you, but perhaps you'd like to see them for yourself?" His eyes swept over me and I could see concern wrinkling his forehead. "At the very least, you could use a little walk in sunlight, I think."

'So it's stopped raining?" I asked.

"There's a chill to the air, but it's stopped raining," he said. "Shall we?"

I kept my art bag with me, but I tucked my flashlight away as we climbed the stone stairs up to the meadow. May was too early for most of the flowers to bloom, but the grass was thick and green after all the rain, waving gently in the breeze and soaking the legs of my pants in the remains of the morning dew before we reached the path through the forest into town.

"My grandmother mentioned family records as well as settlement ones," I said as we walked. "Yrsa was dressed as a volva, but she's not of our family. But should we have her family records too?"

"I already have those for you," he assured me. "The family brought them over at my request this morning. But there is nothing there beyond what we have in the settlement records. Her disappearance was never solved at the time, you know, and there were precious few clues as to what even *might* have happened."

I nodded, but I knew there was something more. He was being too withdrawn. Like something he had read had disturbed him. "Do you have a suspicion I should know about?" I asked when the silence had stretched on too long.

"Hm? Not about the disappearance," he said. "No, I worry about Vali. The entries in the family book are all by his mother at the time of the disappearance and then on until her death. After that, it was his younger sister for a few decades until she, too, passed. Now it's been her oldest daughter, Vali's niece, for the last few years."

"Okay…" I said, not following what was bothering him at all.

"They don't mention Vali much," he went on. "His mother noted he was upset at the time, but that's understandable. Then a year later, when the family had a sort of memorial service for her, he was mentioned only briefly as still being grief-struck. 'As if not a moment had passed.' That's how she described it."

"He seems grief-struck to this day," I said, remembering his anger the day before. "If he's truly been working this curse since then, it all tracks."

"Yes," Haraldr said. "I couldn't point to any one thing in any part of their family book, but the weight of it all together is three generations of women who are carefully not recording a thing he's doing. The comings and goings of every other member of their family are written down in almost exhaustive detail. But all three of them chose to simply not speak of Vali."

"Were they afraid of him, do you think?" I asked.

"Someone nursing a grudge for a century must be very hard to live with," he said. We were nearly through the village now, approaching the door to his house.

"Are you trying to tell me that giving Vali closure about his sister will be a good thing for the rest of his family?" I asked as we climbed the steps to his door. "Because, if there was a way to set his mind at ease without unleashing this curse he's been nursing for years, I would take it in a heartbeat."

"I've already spoken to your grandmother," Haraldr told me. "While you are solving this murder, she is working on figuring out if Vali has the power to do what he threatens. By the time you have your answer, hopefully she will have hers as well. Then we on the council can decide what should be done."

"Good," I said. "If he has an artifact, we definitely need to know."

"Nora intends to rule that out first," Haraldr said.

Then we were in his library. The midday sun streamed in diffusely, lighting up the room without ever touching any of the books directly. He led me to a table where two books were resting. One was sitting closed, but various strips of paper were poking out of it, doubtless marking key passages.

The other was sitting open to a point about two-thirds of the way through its many pages. The paper was yellowed with age, and of so coarse a make I could see bits of wood pulp visible within it. The ink had faded with time as well, what once had been black now a watery gray in all too many places.

Plus, it was all written in Villmark Norse. I was better with the native tongue of my new home than I had been when I first entered Haraldr's library, but I still was far from fluent.

And this was Villmark Norse from a century ago. Just a brief scan showed me the writer of this text still used the capitalized "They" for a more formal "you." I was sure that was not the only archaic phrase that was going to slow me down.

"Don't worry. I'm here," Haraldr said, as if reading my mind. "This other book is the family history. I've told you enough about that for your purposes, but it is there as a reference if you feel you need it later."

"And this one?" I said, touching the open book.

"The official settlement history," Haraldr said. "Of course, there is not just one book for everything that happens within Villmark. There are separate books to record births, deaths, marriages and divorces from economic and trade matters. This particular text only records crimes or potential crimes. Thefts are rare in Villmark, as you likely know. Murder is less so, but that is only truly considered a crime when it is hidden. If it is confessed to and the blood price is paid, the matter is considered closed. And you'll see a mark like this one here."

He flipped back a few pages and pointed to a sigil like from a signet ring, only in ink and not wax. It looked like a double-bladed axe.

"Kind of like the sword of justice?" I asked, touching the symbol with a fingertip. "It cuts both ways?"

"Perhaps," Haraldr said. "It dates back to the oldest of disputes in our records. I assume we brought that symbol here from Old Norway. But some things are lost to the oceans of time."

"So how much is known about Yrsa's case?" I asked.

"That starts on this page," he said, turning back to where it had stood open before. "This was written after the search had ended, as a sort of record of everything known before the guardians at the time just gave up."

"Like a cold case file," I said, flipping through the pages. There were only four, but the handwriting was very dense. And even a cursory scan told me the old Villmarker Norse was going to be a tough read. "The point of bringing me here was a walk in the sun, right?" I reminded him.

He laughed. "I can see you were up all night, so I'll have a little mercy for your tired brain," he said, taking the book from me. He skimmed over the text briefly, then turned back to the beginning. "I'll sum up for you."

"Thank you," I said, and the two of us took our customary seats by his fireplace.

"Yrsa was about twenty when she disappeared. She was very popular and quite beautiful," he said. "Twenty was a bit old at that time to still be unmarried, but it wasn't for lack of prospects. She turned down several offers, but her parents weren't quite at the point of despair."

"Was she just being picky, or do you think something else was going on?" I asked.

"The records don't say," he admitted, flipping through the pages as if to be sure.

"Because she was dressed as a volva," I reminded him. "Was she training with the volva at the time?"

"There is definitely no record of that, and there would have been," he said. "But even if she *did* aspire to pursue the life of a volva, that doesn't necessarily preclude marriage."

"But it would be unusual?" I pressed. He had lingered over the word "necessarily" just a touch too long.

"Your mother married, of course," he said.

"But she left the volva life behind when she did so," I countered.

"Only because she left all of Villmark behind."

"Was my grandmother ever married?" I asked.

"I'm quite sure I am *not* the one you should be asking that question," he said primly.

"Fine," I said with a shrug. "So, beautiful maiden Yrsa who kept turning down marriage proposals disappears. What does the record say?"

"She was last seen at someone else's wedding party, a friend of hers," he said, apparently happy to be back to summarizing the book for me. "The party lasted all through the night to the next morning. Some people slept, but others were up carousing all night long. No one knows exactly when Yrsa was seen last. She had been one of the bride's maidens and had been sitting at the high table during the feasting. And she was seen dancing for quite some time. But when dawn came, no one could find her."

"And no one saw her leaving the party or anything obviously suspicious, I'm guessing?" I said.

"At first it was thought she had just had too much mead and had wandered off, then fallen asleep somewhere," he said. "The entire village was searched. Then it was feared that, again, she had wandered away from the others, but some creature from beyond the village borders had carried her off. Such things happened on occasion. So all the wilds to the north and west were searched. But there was no sign of her there either."

"And the caves were searched," I said.

"Yes. Although no one had any reason to think she was down there," Haraldr said, his finger scanning over the lines. "Yes, it was just to be thorough they were searched."

"And yet that's where she was. If only they could've been more thorough." Not that I was accusing them of negligence. I had spent an entire night trying to find what they had missed, with no more luck than they had had.

"The guardian who wrote the entry took one final step," Haraldr said as he carefully turned a brittle page. "He made a record of everyone who was seen speaking with Yrsa during the wedding party."

"Wouldn't that be most of the village?" I asked.

"Yes, but there were three in particular who he focused on most strongly," he said. "Three men who each proposed to her that very night and were turned down."

"And didn't take it well?" I guessed.

"I would certainly never counsel a young man to make a public proposal when he wasn't sure of a positive response," Haraldr said. "And in this case, each of the proposals came late in the evening, after everyone had had their share of mead and ale."

"But nothing ever came of investigating these three, right?" I asked.

"The guardian at the time could find no proof of anything, nothing more than suspicion," Haraldr said, turning to the last page of the entry. "But when he closed the case, it was clear he was deeply unsatisfied. He was sure that Yrsa had met a bad end at one of their hands. Only he couldn't decide which of the three felt the most guilty to him. Only that they definitely never would've acted together. So he had to let the whole matter go. To his torment."

"Maybe I can discern more of the story than he could," I said, without a lot of hope. A hundred years was a lot of time. And yet, so far as I knew, my ability to draw what had happened in the past had no particular limit.

"I thought that might be what you'd say," Haraldr said with a faint smile. "Something else that will set your mind at ease, perhaps, is that like Vali and Yrsa, none of them have any direct descendants. Like Vali, they never married or had children of their own. But their siblings did."

"Vali is as likely to curse grandnieces and -nephews as grandchildren, isn't he?" I said.

"I'm afraid so," Haraldr said. "And the blood price will still be owed. But if one of them actually did this thing, at least they died without issue themselves. It helps with the family hamingja that they had no children."

"If they were even guilty in the first place," I said. "If they didn't work together, then at least two of them were innocent, if not all three."

"Let's hope you can find out what happened and we can set all things to rights," Haraldr said. "The first of the suspects was a man named Lodvik. He would've been the older brother of Loke and Esja's great-grandfather."

I sucked in a breath. Until that minute, it hadn't occurred to me that the family owing the blood price, the family facing Vali's curse, could be a family I knew so well.

But I nodded for Haraldr to go on. He gave me a look of sympathy, then said, "the second was a man named Grimmunder. He was the younger brother of Kara and Nilda's great-great-grandmother."

This was just getting better and better. I pressed a shaking hand to my forehead, but again nodded for Haraldr to continue.

"The third was a man named Rolfr. He was the older brother of Valki's grandfather," Haraldr said.

Which made him the older brother of Thorbjorn's great-grandfather.

I was really starting to regret promising to take on this work. If any one of the three of them were the guilty party, I was about to bring a lot of misery down on one of my friends.

"What happens if I don't get an answer?" I asked.

"If there is no answer to be found, the blood price will remain unpaid," Haraldr said. "That would leave two families' hamingja in a state of disorder. I would certainly hope you would do everything you could to avert such a thing."

"But what do you think Vali would do?" I asked.

"I think what I'm sure you're thinking," Haraldr said. "Vali knows his life is at its end. He's only lived so long out of stubbornness, nursing that curse. If you told him you had no name to give him, he will likely curse all three families. And likely you as well."

"I can handle myself," I said.

But there was no way I was going to let him hurt any of my friends.

Hopefully, my grandmother would find a way to stop his curse.

In the meantime, I had a job to do. And I knew just which family to start with.

The one that seemed cursed already.

Loke and Esja Grímsson.

CHAPTER TWELVE

If any family's hamingja seemed cursed by the hidden, bad actions of an ancestor, it was the Grímssons'.

Loke and Esja had lost their parents to a house fire when they were both still young kids. He was cursed with randomly being pulled through portals when he stepped through doorways. And his sister was plagued with a chronic illness that I wasn't sure if anyone had even tried to diagnose.

So after bidding Haraldr farewell, I headed south, downhill from Villmark to the collection of dairy farms that clustered there. The road became a track of wagon wheels, and where I turned off that track, I followed what was little more than a footpath.

But that path led into a hollow nestled between two ridges of rolling green hills dotted with grazing cows.

Then I saw the house, still a jarring sight.

The village of Villmark had a few old Norse buildings of timber and thatch, or logs with sod roofs. But most of the homes were surprisingly modern. The flat lines, modern materials, and large glass windows would fit right in the pages of any current issue of a Scandinavian architecture magazine.

Runde, on the other hand, was thoroughly northern Minnesotan, farmhouses from the mid-century and fish houses that were even older. I know I have a biased eye, but the town looks like it never quite escaped the Great Depression.

The Grímsson home looked like neither of these things. No, this house had no business being nestled among cow fields, and yet there it was, in all its English Gothic manor glory, pointy corner towers and all.

I knocked on the door and was surprised to find it answered right away, and by both siblings. They shared a resemblance in being almost painfully thin and pale, but where Loke had chocolate-brown hair and eyes, Esja was blonde with cornflower blue eyes. But she was looking well today, with a little pink bloom to her cheeks.

And she was definitely happy to see me.

"Were you two waiting for me?" I asked.

"Everyone has heard about Yrsa, the woman whose body you found," Loke said with a careless shrug.

"We know our family's history," Esja said. "We figured you would be here to ask us about it."

"So you know about Lodvik," I said.

"We know about Lodvik," Loke said. I didn't realize I was hovering uncertainly on the doorstep until he reached out to pull me into the dark interior of their front hall.

"I've pulled out everything we have about our..." she trailed off and gave Loke a questioning look.

"Great-grandfather's older brother, I believe," Loke said.

"That's what Haraldr told me," I said. "He never married and had no children of his own?"

"That's right," Esja said. "But that's not unusual in our family." She sighed. "Our family tree is practically just a stunted trunk."

"Esja has everything in the library," Loke said to me. "Esja, lead the way."

But when she swept up the hall towards a set of double-doors on the right side of the marble checkerboard floor, Loke caught my elbow to delay me long enough to whisper close to my ear. "What happens with me is nothing to do with what Lodvik did. Just so we're clear."

"I thought Mjolner and I broke the spell that kept you telling me what was going on with you," I said.

"You did. This is just me not being in a sharing place," he said with a wicked grin. "What is happening with me is all my doing. As I've told you."

"You said it's been happening to you since you were a kid," I reminded him.

"All my doing," he repeated, emphasizing each word distinctly. "It's not a curse passed down through my family."

"And Esja?" I asked him.

He had been about to head towards the library, but he did a double-take at my question.

Clearly, he had never considered that before.

"Are you coming?" Esja called from beyond the open doors.

"Coming," Loke called back. He gave me a quick shake of his head, but whether he meant that he didn't think Esja was sick because of his family's owed blood price, or whether he meant he didn't want me to discuss it in front of her, I wasn't sure.

Maybe he wasn't either.

We went into the library where Esja was sitting by a roaring fire inside of an elaborately carved, if decidedly dirty, marble fireplace.

The breeze outside was still chilly, but that fire was so warm that I moved the other chair back a couple of feet before I sat down to see what Esja had arrayed on the little table in front of her.

There were photographs. Actual sepia-colored photographs. I hadn't expected that. Although I probably should have. The youth of Villmark today, half of them had cellphones in their pockets. Back in the 1920s, I bet they had cameras hidden under their beds.

"This is Lodvik on the left, next to our great-grandfather," Esja said, handing one of the photographs to me. It was two men dressed like northern Minnesotan farmers of the 1920s in faded wool trousers and work shirts with the sleeves rolled up to their elbows.

The man on the left, the older of the two, was like a strange cross between Loke and Thorbjorn. He had all of Loke's dark looks and devilish charm that came through even in such a stilted, posed photo. But he was tall and broad in the shoulders, with arms so thick I doubted the cuffs would button around those wrists even if he did roll the sleeves back down.

I had no idea dairy farmers could get so buff. Had he bench-pressed cows? Or was that just from lifting those heavy milk cans back in the day?

"He loved Yrsa with all his heart," Esja said with an "isn't it romantic?" sort of sigh.

"Apparently," Loke was compelled to add. He was standing behind my chair with his arms folded, looking over my shoulder at the photo in my hands.

"We have his *letters*," Esja said, shifting some things aside to hand me a packet of worn tri-folded papers all tied up in a faded blue ribbon. "I guess she sent them all back, and that's how they ended up here with the rest of his things. He never loved again." She let out another wistful sigh.

"We don't know that," Loke said. "It's not like he kept a journal or anything. We looked, but there was nothing. Just those letters, returned but apparently opened and read at some point."

"He never married," Esja said firmly.

"He died young," Loke said.

"Of a broken heart."

"Of *influenza*," Loke said. I turned in my chair to look up at him and he rolled his eyes.

"Be nice," I admonished him.

"I really wished we could've found more, but there really isn't much here," Esja sighed. "Probably not helpful in your investigation."

'A journal might have been interesting, but people lie in journals too,' I said.

"He had a room in the attic that survived the fire," Loke said. "His bed is gone, but he slept there every day of his life. Maybe that left an imprint you can sense now."

"I see you have your drawing things with you," Esja said shyly.

"I do," I agreed. "Would you like to draw with me? Perhaps you will sense things I don't. He *is* your ancestor, after all."

"Really?" Esja asked, clasping her hands together.

"It's chilly up there, Esja," Loke said. "If you're going to be up there to draw, put on your warmer socks and boots and a coat. I'll fetch a blanket, and you'll need a chair."

"Don't fuss over me, Loke!" she protested.

"You're not sitting on the floor!" he shouted back at her.

"Get some layers on," I said to her. "I'll wait until you're ready."

She gave me a grateful smile, her brother an exasperated look, then swept out of the room to do as she was told.

"She seems much better than the last time I saw her," I said to him in a low voice.

"She has good days and bad days," he said almost absently, like his mind was somewhere else. Then he fixed me with a steady gaze. "This is a good day."

"I'm not going to do anything to change that," I promised him.

"Do you really think having her there will help you?" he asked.

"Of course. His blood is in her blood. And yours," I said.

"Oh, I'll be there," he assured me. "I can't trust you to watch out for Esja. Not if you're going to be *drawing*."

"Yeah, if I do go into a fugue state, I should probably have you there to kick me back out of it," I admitted.

Esja came back even more bundled up than Loke had told her to be. She had a hat pulled lower over her ears, a coat buttoned up high on her neck, and even a pair of fingerless gloves on her hands. She was also clutching a pad of sketch paper close to her chest.

But she was practically dancing with excitement.

Loke led the way upstairs. Most of the homes in Villmark didn't have anything like an attic. The flat roofs didn't accommodate them. But this Gothic-style house had a complex of warrens that ran throughout the attic, narrow but tall spaces over the main body of the house, with wider openings over the tower rooms.

But the ceilings in the spaces over the tower rooms sloped severely from peaks in the center down to the floorboards, with nothing you'd really call a wall anywhere. The few windows were low, serving more to illuminate the dust on the floor than anything else.

And none of the rooms had doors. There was a staircase that led up through a trapdoor, then everything else was only separated by twists and turns. And half of the space still had fire damage, letting the wind blow through. The fire that had burned the wall of the first floor study and the entirety of their parents' bedroom had consumed nearly half of the attic. And only rudimentary repairs had been done to the roof. The rooms below were merely left as they were, behind locked doors.

Loke hadn't been joking that it would be cold up here. I hoped it wouldn't take long to find what I needed through sketching.

"This was his childhood room?" I asked when I realized the space over the tower we were standing in was our final destination.

"It was his room his entire life," Loke said.

"Sleeping here as a heartbroken adult is one thing. But who would put a kid up here?" I said with a shiver that had nothing to do with the spring air blowing through without the touch of sunlight to temper its chill.

"I gather he chose it," Loke said. "Some of us are loners by nature."

"No one in this room, I shouldn't think," Esja said with a sly smile at her brother. He set the folding chair he was carrying as close to the light from one of the windows as he could manage and she settled into it. Then she allowed him to tuck a fur-lined blanket all around her legs.

I just sat down on the floor, about where I imagined a bed would be. But there was no sign that there had ever been any furniture in this room. No mar on the wood panels that constituted the floor, no uneven fading from differing exposures to sunlight. Nothing.

Loke retreated a bit, back towards the center of the house, but Esja and I were both already engrossed in our work.

I was surprised how much it felt like I knew him already, Lodvik, a man I had never met and had only seen briefly in a single photograph. But there had been something in his eyes.

I just knew Esja was right. He had loved Yrsa, and when she had turned him down, he had never managed to carry on.

But the sketches that grew under my moving pencil told a slightly different story. He hadn't withered away because she had failed to love him. I could see in the body language of the figure I was drawing, a figure that paced this room throughout the long hours of the night when he could never find sleep.

He had known she would never love him. All she had done by turning down his proposal was confirm it.

But she had disappeared without a trace. Without anyone knowing her fate. And every day that passed without anyone discovering what had happened to her had been like another weight in the invisible bag of unrelenting sadness he carried. Until that weight had just crushed him.

I didn't realize I was weeping until Loke stepped close to me to offer me a handkerchief. One of Esja's, to judge by the lacy trim.

"Sorry," I said, wiping at my face.

"I felt it too, I think," Esja said, looking over her own drawings. "There's such sadness in this room, isn't there?"

"He didn't know what to do," I said, retracing one of my own sketches with a graphite-smudged fingertip. "She was gone, and he was alone, and he didn't know how to fix it."

"It's getting late," Loke said. "There's soup in the kitchen, and a fire. Let's go get warmed up."

"I should go," I said, shoving my sketchbook back in my bag. "But thank you for your help."

"You're welcome back if you need to learn more," Esja said. Then she tore a stack of pages out of her sketchbook and handed them to me. "In case they can help you."

"Thank you," I said.

As she fussed with putting her things away, Loke took my arm and drew me far enough away to whisper close to my ear.

"Do you think he did it? Do you think that's why Esja…"

He couldn't finish the thought, largely because Esja was standing up now and looking over at the two of us.

"I don't know. But I promise I'll find out."

He nodded, satisfied.

In a way, I almost wished it had been Lodvik who had killed Yrsa. If paying a blood price would be all it took to make Esja well again, I knew Loke would gladly pay.

But a part of me was worried. Lodvik was feeling a little cursed to me, too. Maybe whatever was wrong with their family had affected him, too.

But that would mean the problem was far older. My work might not yet be done here.

For now, though, I had to call on the Mikkelsens.

CHAPTER THIRTEEN

I REACHED the Mikkelsen house door at midafternoon. The air was still cool, but the sun was starting to dry up the rain. The gutters were still chattering streams of running water, but the cobblestones were mostly dry, as were the occasional shrubs and plants that brushed against me as I passed.

Again, my knock was answered before I had quite finished rapping the door with my knuckles. A couple in their fifties were both standing there, smiling welcomingly at me.

"We've never actually met, have we?" the woman said. She had laugh lines all around her gray eyes and her thick hair, if a darker shade of blonde than either of her daughters', was untouched by any strands of silver. "I'm Laufey."

"Ingrid Torfudottir, pleased to meet you," I said, hiking my art bag higher on my shoulder before shaking her hand.

"Afli Mikkelsen," the man said, closing his large hand around mine. Despite the palpable strength there, he didn't squeeze my hand to death, just gave it a warm clasp, then let me go. His dark hair and eyes were nothing at all like his daughters', but I could see their features in the shapes of his face, and especially in his blacksmith-worthy arms.

"We know why you're here, of course," Laufey said as she guided me inside, to the sunny west-facing sitting room. They were not quite at the edge of the village, but were on a rise above the homes further out, and had an impressive view of the outskirts of Villmark and the rolling forested hills beyond.

"Word travels fast," I said as I sat down on their sofa. The two sat together on the chair opposite me, Afli in the seat and Laufey perched on the wide arm. They settled in with such familiarity I had a feeling they sat just like that a lot. Since that chair faced the windows behind me, they had the better view than me.

I turned my attention to the objects arranged on the coffee table between us. More sepia-colored photographs and scraps of letters as well as a leather-bound book I was sure was the family history.

"Grimmunder was from your side of the family, correct?" I said to Laufey as I reached for one of the photographs.

"That's correct. He was my..." but she trailed off, getting up from the arm of the chair to open the family record book. Just inside the front cover was an elaborately illustrated family tree. It started out with many spreading branches, but the top of the tree was decidedly stunted.

"I'm the last of my line," she told me, pointing to her own name alone on the top-most branch. Only two names were above hers: Nilda and Kara. "Most of Villmark only tracks the paternal line, save of course the Torfudottirs. Many in Villmark wouldn't even consider this book an official family record after the time of Grimmunder's parents."

I followed her fingertip as it traced back past her mother, a lone branch ending only in Laufey, then her mother's mother, also with only a single daughter following, then one more branch up until finally her great-grandmother had a single sibling: Grimmunder.

Who had had no children to match her solitary daughter.

'Before their time, there were many children," Laufey said with a vaguer gesture at the thick foliage below that point.

"Do you think that's significant?" I asked. It was certainly unusual. Just a casual glance showed most of the couples had raised five or six children a piece. The two was break enough. Then the rest of the tree was really just a stick, until Laufey's two daughters.

She gave Afli a nervous glance.

"We agreed we could trust her," he said, looking more blacksmith than ever as he crossed his arms across his broad chest. "She is from the modern world. She will understand."

"Even the girls don't know," Laufey said, although whether to me or to her husband, I wasn't quite sure.

"If you kept something secret from them for a good reason, I would not feel compelled to break that confidence now," I said. I didn't exactly want to promise I wouldn't say a word. Not without knowing what was really going on.

But I was dying to know what had Laufey so nervous. And how it could possibly relate to the crime I was investigating from a century before.

"Both of our daughters were born outside of Villmark," Laufey said. Her cheeks flushed, like she was confessing to an enormous transgression.

But I couldn't see what it was. "Okay," I said slowly. "Do you mean in the north, or...?"

"In Duluth," Afli said, pronouncing the word carefully. Well, it was foreign to most of Villmark.

"Why were you in Duluth?" I asked.

"You understand, this tree only measures the live births," Laufey said. "Not the miscarriages. Not the stillbirths. Even if the mother named them, they don't go into this book."

I nodded. It was sad, but I knew they weren't entirely forgotten. The settlement books recorded everyone, live birth or not. Their names were written. Just not here. But I couldn't help asking. "Why?"

"It would be so much more cluttered, you see," Laufey said. "Especially since Grimmunder's time. My own mother should've had six names after hers, not just mine."

"It was always a problem in the family," Afli said. Laufey was still looking down at the book, but he had caught hold of her hand at her side and was squeezing it tight. "We knew it before we married."

"The girls don't know," Laufey said, and gave me a desperate look.

"Oh," I said, as too many things fell into place at once. "You were in Duluth *because* you were pregnant. To give birth in a hospital. Right?"

"We stayed there for the last trimester, both times. Just to be sure," Afli said. "We told everyone Laufey was on bed rest in her mother's home. There are many who would look down on us for leaving Villmark for such a reason, you understand."

"You ended up with two healthy daughters. I definitely don't see a downside to that," I said. Although I could only imagine how strange it had been for the two of them, alone in a strange place where they barely spoke the language, terrified for the fate of their baby-to-be.

"Two pregnancies and two babies," Laufey said with a hint of pride.

"But you have to tell Kara," I said as apologetically as I could. "Before her wedding. She should know. Like you did."

"We were hoping we wouldn't have to," Afli said with a glance at his wife, who nodded her agreement.

"No, you definitely have to," I said.

"Not if you help us," Afli said. "If it was the actions of this ancestor of Laufey's, of Kara's and Nilda's, if there's a blood price owed, we have to pay it. For their sakes."

I chewed at my lip uncertainly. I would have to ask Haraldr if the two things could even be related, blood prices owed and miscarriages. But I had a sinking feeling I already knew what he'd say.

"You have to tell her either way," I said. "In case he isn't the one who killed Yrsa. If something else is causing the problem."

"They never found anything medically wrong with me," Laufey said.

"Still. She has to know," I said.

"We will tell her," Afli promised. "But we still need to know if this man sullied the family's hamingja through his misdeeds."

I picked up one of the photographs and looked at it. Like the photo of Lodvik, it was a superficially unremarkable photograph of a northern Minnesotan man from the 1920s. Only this one was leaning against a battered old truck with the words "Runde Dairy" painted on the side.

"Do you have anything that connected him to Yrsa?" I asked. "Diaries or letters or anything like that?"

"No, this is all we found about him at all," Laufey said. "After she disappeared, when the searches were halted and life went on without her for the rest of Villmark, he left the village. He went out to my family's hunting lodge and lived out the rest of his days there."

"Did he die young?" I asked.

"Not at all," she said. "Actually, he died shortly after Nilda was born. Not that long ago at all. But I had never met him. My family stopped going out to the lodge when he moved out there."

"Your grandmother and mother both went to the lodges of their husbands' families," Afli reminded her.

"How did he die?" I asked.

"We don't really know," Laufey admitted. "We don't know for sure precisely when he *did* die. People who lived in lodges near him saw him from time to time, but no one knows just who saw him last. He was alone most of the time. And when he was finally missed, my father rode out to check on him. He found the lodge burned to the ground. Grimmunder had been inside at the time. But he might've been dead already."

I nodded, but I knew we were all thinking the same thing. He had been dead already, or he had started the fire himself.

But surely not out of guilt for something he may or may not have done to Yrsa. Not after so many decades. It didn't make sense.

"Is there anything left of the structure now?" I asked.

"Nothing but a few stones from the fireplace," Laufey said. "Maybe not even that, anymore. I haven't been out there in twenty years."

"That's a shame. That would definitely be the spot that left the strongest impression," I said. "I can try sketching by where his bones lie now, but I think where he dwelled during life would be better. But if the place has changed so much..."

I was debating which would be a better use of my time, or rather, which I should try first. If I didn't get anything at one place, I'd have to try the other. I'd have to keep sketching until I had something to go on.

"He grew up here, in this house," Laufey said suddenly.

"Really?" I said. I tried to hide my skepticism, but not particularly successfully. It wasn't strange that they were living in her family's home and not Afli's, especially as she was the sole remaining member of her family.

It was just the house didn't look like it had been around in the 1920s. The windows were modern glass and steel, just to start with.

"I know it doesn't look all that old, but my parents had the entire place rebuilt when I was a child," Laufey said. "The surface features are new, but the bones are old."

"And the rooms are the same?" I asked. Maybe a childhood room would tell me something. Especially if, like Lodvik, it had still been his room when he had had his heart broken by Yrsa.

"No, a lot of the interior walls were moved," she admitted, and my brief bubble of optimism burst. "But I can show you where he spent a lot of his time."

"What do you mean?" I asked.

"The roof is the same, and there is a particular point where the roof that slants down off the back bedrooms meets the roof slanting down from the great room," she said, pointing in the general area somewhere over our heads. I could see the vaulted ceiling above, but had no sense of where it might meet another slope.

"It's clearer when you're up there," Afli said.

"He was something of a poet, apparently," Laufey said. "Or at least the family records say so. None of his poetry survived. I suppose he had it with him at the lodge, and all of it was lost in the fire. But as a teenager and youth, he used to like to sit up there to write as he watched the sunset."

"Show me," I said, getting up at once, gripping my art bag tight in my hands.

I followed them up to the second floor, then to the end of the corridor, past the bedroom doors to a small balcony that overlooked their front garden. There was a metal trellis set against the northern wall of the balcony, the beginning shoots of something viny just starting to climb the bottom rungs.

"It's just up there," Laufey said, pointing to where the two roofs met at the top of the trellis. It certainly made a sturdy ladder.

"I'm sure you need to be alone for your magical work," Afli said to me. "I'll just leave this door open. If you need anything, just call."

"Thank you," I said. I waited for the two of them to go back inside before climbing the trellis.

At first, I was afraid this wasn't going to work. It was clearly modern roofing I was sitting on, not the same substance that Grimmunder had sat on at all.

But then I looked out over the hills to the west. I could see the exact notch between two hills where I knew the sun would touch as it set in a few hours.

I took out my sketchbook and got to work.

CHAPTER FOURTEEN

I STAYED up on the Mikkelsen roof until the sun touched the horizon, but it didn't feel necessary to stay through the sunset itself. Like with Lodvik, I had dozens of sketches that told me all about a lonely man who felt misunderstood, but who just didn't feel like a killer to me.

Grimmunder had built Yrsa up in his mind as a sort of poetic ideal, his muse, as much as I still hated that concept. I don't think Grimmunder totally believed in it either, actually. I think he just really wanted to. He wasn't happy with his own poetic efforts, and he was sure winning the love of his muse would turn that around for him.

I was pretty sure all it would take was time and practice. More words. He had been younger when Yrsa disappeared than I was now. Too young to give up. Especially considering he had been writing poetry in his spare time, when he wasn't bringing milk from the cow farms of Villmark down to Runde to sell to the larger markets.

I felt his sadness and frustration, but it was all inwardly-directed. And when Yrsa disappeared, he had given up on all of it.

I really hoped he had kept writing poetry, living alone out in the woods. But I was pretty sure he hadn't.

So I was sniffling again as I put my sketchbook and supplies away, and realized I still had Esja's handkerchief in my pocket. I mopped at my cheeks before climbing back down.

As I feared, the two Mikkelsens were waiting for me downstairs with expectant faces.

"I don't have anything clear-cut," I told them, not showing them my sketches. "I have more work to do, some other leads to follow up. I might need to go back up there, although right now I don't think so."

"I can take you out to the remains of the hunting lodge, if that would help," Afli offered.

"I'll keep that in mind," I said. "Right now, I want to get to Valki's house before the day is gone entirely. Tell Nilda and Kara that I said hello."

"We will," Laufey said, shaking my hand again. A little too earnestly. I guessed she was letting me know she would tell Kara about the family's struggles with infertility.

I was happy to leave that unsaid myself. But I couldn't stop thinking about it as I headed through the darkening cobblestoned streets, back to the center of town and then up the northern road to the very top end of the village.

If by finding Lodvik was the killer I could cure or at least relieve Esja's condition, that would be a good thing. But so would finding Grimmunder guilty and removing the specter of infertility from Kara and Nilda's family. But they couldn't both be guilty.

And I was really dreading talking to Valki. What if his family too was struggling with some secret they hoped paying an owed blood price would relieve? It didn't seem likely. Being the father of the Thors, being a member of the council of three after a long career as a guardian himself... It was hard to imagine any of that being possible without the family having a strong hamingja.

They were lucky, well-liked, honorable and heroic. Those were all traits associated with good hamingja.

No, I decided as I walked up to their front gate, this was definitely going to be the easy part of the three investigations I was running. There was just no way Valki's ancestor could be the one. All the signs pointed against it.

I could smell roasting elk the minute I passed through their gate. By the time I reached the front door, roasting potatoes and beets were added to the mix. And fresh-baked rye bread loaded with caraway seeds.

I hadn't eaten all day. And I had had little but MREs for days. My stomach gave a rumble of ecstasy just from the smell. But there was an edge to that rumble. My stomach was never going to forgive me if I walked away without filling it first.

This time, I had to knock twice before I got an answer. Then Valki's wife Gunna appeared, wiping her hands on her stained apron. Her cheeks were flushed, and I guessed I had just brought her away from a roaring fire or even an oven.

"Is this a bad time?" I asked, taking half a step back. If any of her sons were home from their patrols, I knew she'd be stuffing them full before sending them out again. That was likely a family moment, one on which I didn't want to intrude.

Of course, it was just possible that Thorbjorn would be one of the ones who was home...

But Gunna crushed that hope before it had even bloomed in my heart. "No, I was just fixing a little dinner for you. I knew you'd be coming. Come in! Valki went into town to deal with a small wedding detail, but he'll be back in time for dinner to speak with you."

I slipped off my shoes then followed her into the kitchen, half in a daze. There was the elk I had smelled, under a tent of foil on a thick wooden cutting board on the center of the kitchen table. Two loaves of bread were wrapped in white cloth, uncut inside the breadbasket. And as I lingered in the doorway, Gunna bustled back into the kitchen to finish spooning potatoes and beets that had roasted to dark caramelly goodness from a sheet pan onto a serving platter.

But there were only three place settings at the table. The larger table was in the dining room beyond, but that room was dark and clearly unoccupied.

"This is all for me?" I asked, twisting the straps of my art bag in my hands as I looked at all the food. I hadn't had proper food in so long.

Pretty much since I had left my grandmother alone in that cabin in the north more than a month before.

"Well, we knew you were coming," Gunna said. "Of course, I always make enough for any of my boys, should they find their way home. Not that I'm expecting any. But I'm never not expecting them either."

"It was like this with Valki when he was a guardian too," I guessed.

"Yes," Gunna said, sucking a bit of potato off the side of her thumb before bringing the platter over to the table. "That's why he's on the council now, you know. I insisted he find a job in town when the boys started going out on patrol themselves. I needed to know where at least one of my menfolk was."

I didn't know what to say to that. I knew that Valki had started taking up guardian duties just since I had been back in town. First watching the ancestral fire behind the waterfall while all of his sons were on patrol, and then more duties when they had disappeared. I was pretty sure my arrival had upset things, but I hadn't appreciated before how that could trickle down even to Gunna.

"It's not so bad as all that," Gunna said, snapping me back out of my reverie.

"I'm sorry?" I said.

"Being married to a guardian," she said. "And now being mother to more. It's a hard life, but I wouldn't trade it for anything."

"No, of course not," I was quick to say.

"Of course, as a volva, you'd have plenty to do to fill your hours," she said, spinning back towards the kitchen to dig through her drawers for a bread knife. "Not that raising those five boys of mine didn't keep my hands full!"

I knew I was gaping at her, but I wasn't sure exactly when this conversation had taken such a sudden turn. Kara was the one who was about to marry one of Gunna's guardian sons, after all, not me.

But then the front door slammed open and then shut again. Gunna dropped the knife on the table near the breadbasket, then hustled out to the hall to greet her husband.

I set my bag in the corner, out of the way, and eased into the chair furthest from the kitchen. This put me with my back to the windows that framed the setting sun; that felt like the spot for guests.

Then Valki and Gunna were back, and Valki started carving the elk as Gunna sliced the bread. The two of them working together loaded up my plate with startling speed.

But I emptied it nearly as fast. I was starving, and the hot food was so good. Delicious and comforting all at once.

Gunna just laughed and refilled my plate. Then she and Valki had a low conversation that was almost in code, just a series of half-questions that were met with half-answers. I gathered they were discussing the errand Valki had just been running, and they both found the outcome satisfactory. I let the words just wash over me as I ate, but it was a warm comfort, too. Basking in their marital shorthand.

"Now, you're here about my grandfather's older brother. Rolfr," Valki said after he had pushed his plate away and turned his attention to the tankard of ale that had sat untouched until now.

"That's correct," I said. "He proposed to Yrsa and was turned down on the night she disappeared. Also, I gather he never married or had children afterwards?"

"Didn't have much opportunity to," Valki said as he wiped foam from his beard and mustache. "He died not long after. Killed by trolls, or so the stories go."

"No one saw it?" I asked.

"My grandfather did," Valki said. "But it wasn't a tale he liked to tell. The record of it in the family book is very brief."

That was downright odd. Such tales were usually the opposite: over-embellished with outrageous details over many, many retellings.

"So he wasn't any kind of artist?" I asked. Valki choked on the ale he had been in the process of swallowing, then gave me a look that bordered on real annoyance. "I take it that's a 'no'?"

"Why would you think he was?" he demanded.

"One of the other suspects, Grimmunder, was a poet," I said. "And Lodvik had an artistic temperament. Or at least I thought so."

"You speak as though you've met them," Valki said.

"I get impressions when I draw," I said, although I knew he knew this. I had explained it to the council before. Thorbjorn had even helped me with my sketches on more than one occasion. He certainly had never looked at me like his father was looking at me now, like I was delusional.

"Ingrid brings different skills to her working than Nora does," Gunna said with the air of a wife reminding her husband of something they've discussed on many occasions.

Valki rolled his eyes, then took another swallow of ale. But after wiping his mouth with his napkin, he gave me a more steady gaze. "Gunna speaks of what happened when you were our guest at her family's hunting lodge, last winter."

Now I was the one swallowing, only I had no ale in my mouth. Only the bile taste of anxiety, and it wouldn't go down.

I had done my best, but it had taken me days to figure out that the Wild Hunt was running through those woods. And that someone was luring the young women in our party out of doors in the middle of the night, luring them straight into the Wild Hunt's path. Two had died before I had figured that out.

It hadn't been one of my finer moments.

"I know that was only a few months ago, but I promise I've gotten much better at my magic since then," I said.

"Oh, my dear," Gunna said, reaching across the table to squeeze both my hands. "You misunderstand me. I don't blame you. Not at all! I'm only reminding my husband of all you did. And, as you say, your skills have only grown since." She let me go and sat back, but gave her husband a hard glare as she added, "and she saved our Kara."

"That she did," Valki said, grudgingly.

"Do you have anything of Rolfr's I can look at?" I asked, eager to get on to the real work. "Photos or diaries or anything?"

"Honestly? Just a few entries in the family book," Valki said.

"Go on," Gunna prompted him.

Valki grumbled and looked down at the bottom of his ale mug. But he didn't take another drink, just set the mug aside. "I've always gotten the feeling that my grandfather considered Rolfr a bit of a coward.

That his own actions led to his death at the hands of those trolls. Trolls are usually not a deadly danger to my family."

"No, I've seen that," I said. And I had. An entire hillside covered in trolls had been easily outmatched by Thorbjorn and his brothers.

"Our family doesn't hold with many modern ways," Valki went on. "No photographs of any of us now, let alone of Rolfr a hundred years ago. And if he left anything personal behind, that was buried with him."

"And this house?" I said, looking around the room hopefully. It all felt woefully modern, but then so had the Mikkelsen house.

But Valki was already shaking his head. "I built this house myself. I only had one brother and one sister, and I let my sister keep the house at the center of town. I needed more room for my family."

"Oh, that was your doing, was it? The big family?" Gunna teased. Considering she had borne the five sons, and her sister had five daughters to match, it did feel like someone else's genetics favored large families.

But Valki just shrugged, the look of pride not dimming on his face even a little.

"So Rolfr grew up in the house in town where your sister lives now?" I asked.

"No, the house he grew up in is long gone, now," Valki said with a frown. "It's a bakery. Her sister's bakery, in point of fact."

Gunna shrugged, then reached for another slice of the rye bread, as if prompted by the very word "bakery" to have more bread.

"So he left nothing behind, and there's no place to be near where he was when he was around?" I asked.

I really hoped I wasn't about to be sent on a quest to find the spot where trolls had killed him. That would definitely have to wait until the next day. There was barely a sliver of sun left in the western sky.

But then Gunna said, "everything that was personal to him, little as it may have been, would be interred with him in the family barrow. Wouldn't it, Valki?"

"I've seen the stone with his name on it," Valki said as he reached for the last of his ale. "I've never moved it. I assume nothing is behind it save his bones." He gave me a challenging look.

"I don't think I'd have to disturb anything," I said in a rush. "I just need to be near where he is. I'm sure that would be enough to get a sense of him. Can you take me to your family barrow?"

"No need for me to take you," he said as he got up from the table. I was afraid he was going to leave the room, but he was only moving to stand behind my chair. I turned to see him gazing out the window behind me. He was pointing at something. "Do you see it there? On top of the last hill before the sun."

"What am I looking for?" I asked, not quite daring to press my face to the glass. "Is there a flag or some kind of marker?"

"No, just a pile of stones," he said.

I squinted, struggling to make out details in the dying light, when the only source of that light was stabbing straight into my eyes.

But I thought I saw it.

"It's about a half hour's walk from here," he said as he turned back to the table. "Perhaps you should wait until morning."

"No, I can find it in the twilight just fine," I said.

I don't know why I felt in such a hurry. Any evidence had already waited a century for discovery. What was another night?

And yet, I didn't want to wait. I said my goodbyes, then hustled through the gloaming, trying to beat the sun.

At least there was one family I could safely hope *wasn't* the culprit. I could take a little comfort in that.

CHAPTER FIFTEEN

IT WAS FULLY dark by the time I climbed the steep hill that I was certain had been the one Valki had pointed out to me. I could see stony protrusions jutting through the grass around me, other family barrows built into the hill itself. I didn't know if there were any sort of hierarchy of families I was strolling through, unaware. But there was only one that stood alone, like a beehive built of stone atop the hill. All the others were out of sight, overgrown by the spring grasses.

Even this one didn't look like it saw many visitors. I had to push the dried remains of last year's grass out of the doorway before I could get inside.

I was instantly grateful I had put my flashlight in my art bag after giving up my hunt for the older ancestral fire. I found it by touch, then shined it around the interior.

It was smaller on the inside than I had expected. But then I realized if the walls contained skeletons, they would have to be quite thick. They weren't wide enough for men as tall as Valki's family members to be stretched out head to toe inside the walls, but they didn't miss that depth by much. Still, I was sure the bones in the walls were in heaps, not stretched out like sleeping figures.

There was a flat stone like a table in the center of the space. I was about to sit on it when I realized this would be where bodies were arranged long ago. Before cremation had become the method of choice, when the bodies would be left out on that table until the flesh fell away from the bones. Only then would the bones go into the walls.

I didn't know if Rolfr had had such a burial, but if the table was there, it had once been used for that purpose. It would be sacrilegious to sit on it.

Instead, I walked slowly around the circular interior, sweeping the walls with my flashlight. The stones that marked where bones were interred were no larger or smaller than any of the others, but they were marked faintly by runes. I found the one marked Rolfr and ran my fingertips over the shapes of the letters of his name.

It didn't feel like anything. No spark of insight or sudden sense of knowing him.

I sat down on the floor before his marker stone, back against the side of the center table, and took out my flashlight. But it quickly became clear that trying to balance the sketchbook on my knees while I drew with one hand and held a flashlight in the other was beyond awkward.

And it was going to be a real impediment to finding my flow state, let alone the fugue state where I found my deepest magic.

I felt a momentary twinge of nervousness, an awareness of the dead bodies all around me. But dead bodies had never meant me any harm. I clicked off the flashlight and set it aside.

Then I started drawing. In my fugue state, I had no awareness of my surroundings, anyway. What use was light in that situation?

I woke to find the first rays of dawn blinding me through the open doorway. But that wasn't what had roused me.

It had been Thorbjorn, shaking my shoulder. Apparently repeatedly, to judge from the worry on his face.

"There you are," he said as I sat up.

"Did I lose days again?" I asked, aghast.

"No, just the one night," he assured me. "I got home about an hour ago, and my father sent me up here to check on you. He never comes up here himself if he can help it."

"I hope I didn't worry your parents," I said, still feeling groggy and disoriented. I saw my flashlight lying on the dirt floor and put it back in my bag. Then I found my sketchbook, mostly under my hip. I had bent the spiral binding under my weight as I slept. If you could call what I had been doing sleep.

"It's okay if you worried me?" he asked.

"Well, you didn't even know anything was going on before you were on your way up here," I said teasingly.

Then I scootched closer to the rising sun to look at what I had drawn the night before.

It wasn't good. No wonder I didn't want to remember it. It was horrifying looking at the images now, realizing I had drawn them while sitting alone in the dark.

"What is all that?" Thorbjorn asked. "Murder and gore? You know, this wasn't a place of sacrifice. Just funerals."

"I know," I said, glancing over my shoulder at the table behind me. "That wasn't where this came from."

"Where, then?" Thorbjorn asked, and I realized he didn't even know why I was up there. I didn't want to look at him, not until I knew what I was going to say.

But not looking at him told him enough. He sat down beside me, shoulder to shoulder, against the stone table with the rising sun before us.

"Tell me," he said.

"Your great-grandfather's older brother was a deeply disturbed man," I said with a sigh.

Thorbjorn touched his fingers as if counting back. "Rolfr?" he guessed at last.

"Rolfr," I agreed, turning from one page of horrific carnage to another. "If it helps, I don't think he did these things. I think he just… fantasized about them."

"No, actually, that doesn't help," Thorbjorn said. "What's this all about?"

"I found a body in the caves under Villmark," I said. "She was killed next to an older ancestral fire, one I'm not sure I can even find again without Mjolner's help."

"I already have so many questions," Thorbjorn said, but didn't ask them. He just waited for me to go on.

"Her name was Yrsa, and she died about a hundred years ago," I said. "She was dressed as a volva, although I don't know why. She wasn't a Torfudottir. She was considered missing in all the settlement records because her body was never found, but the guardian at the time suspected three men of possibly being involved with whatever happened to her. Rolfr was one of them."

"How did she die?" Thorbjorn asked.

I turned back a few pages and showed him a charcoal sketch of a woman on her knees, her hands tied behind her back, as a man stood over and behind her with a rock raised high, about to strike her down.

"Pretty much like this, only her hands weren't tied when we found her," I said.

"So he did it," he said. "He killed her."

"Honestly? I'm not sure," I said. "Look, most of these are clearly fantasies. Here, he's defeating legions of men, all with swords. This one has a dragon. And this one has a trio of trolls. Only that was how he died, Rolfr. He was killed by trolls. Your great-grandfather saw him die."

"I know the tale," Thorbjorn said. "It's not one we tell at feasts and festivals, that's for sure. But I always got the impression that my father thought Rolfr had... not exactly killed himself, but took on a fight he knew he wouldn't win."

"I got that sense too, from your father," I said. "Now... I wonder."

"What do you wonder?" Thorbjorn asked, taking the sketchbook from my hands and closing it firmly. I felt the same way. No more perusing those sketches. Ever.

"I wonder if your great-grandfather knew there was something wrong with Rolfr," I said. I realized I was whispering, although the only people who could possibly overhear us there were the dead.

And I've heard they tell no tales.

"You think he was afraid Rolfr might do some of these things, and just got rid of him while out on patrol?" Thorbjorn asked. But not disbelievingly.

"Or he feared Rolfr already had. With Yrsa, for example," I said.

"No, that I don't believe," he said firmly.

"It's possible. He certainly seems to have had the mental and emotional capacity," I said.

"No, I don't doubt that Rolfr could be the killer you're looking for," he said. "I doubt that my great-grandfather, if he suspected it, would deal with it like that. On his own, away from the village."

"In secret," I finished for him. "Yes, that's the problem. Because the whole reason I'm even trying to solve this century-old murder is because Yrsa's younger brother wants the blood price paid."

"And so it should be," Thorbjorn said. "If my great-grandfather killed Rolfr to cover up this crime, that's bad for the whole family."

"Believe me, I've had that lesson many times in the last few days," I sighed. "I still don't like it. It still doesn't feel fair."

"I won't explain it to you again, then," he said. "I'll only say, if that price is owed, and it's my family that owes it, you'll be doing us a boon by telling us so."

"I know," I said. "The thing is, the other two suspects are from families that actually feel like something like bad hamingja is clouding them. Only those suspects don't feel guilty to me the way your ancestor does."

"If there was a coverup, they could all be part of it," Thorbjorn said after a long moment's thought. "No matter what happens next, getting it all out into the light is unquestionably a good thing. You have to do it, Ingrid."

"I know," I said. "I just don't know what to do next. I'm afraid I'm going to let everyone down."

And I hadn't even told him the part about Vali's looming curse.

I really hoped my grandmother was making more progress than I was.

"I think I know what you need to do next," Thorbjorn said suddenly.

"Oh, what's that?" I asked. My eyes had slipped closed again. Falling unconscious after drawing furiously through a fugue state was *not* like sleeping, I reminded myself yet again. I was so very tired.

But there was a smile in Thorbjorn's voice when he said, "you need to go back down to that older ancestral fire."

"I thought I told you, I can't find it on my own," I said. I just wanted to snuggle against the warmth of the wool cloak that was draped over his shoulder and sleep for a hundred years. What difference would another hundred years make?

"I know. It's just, your guide is here," he said, that smile in his voice brighter than ever.

I opened my eyes, just a slit, but there was no mistaking it. It was Mjolner's outline, standing between me and the pink rays of the morning sun.

"Now?" I moaned.

Mjolner's answering meow sounded a lot like the word "now." It also sounded very scolding. Like I was a kid he was trying to get out of bed before I missed the school bus.

"I just want to stay here," I said stubbornly.

"As much as I'd love to spend a few hours with you sleeping against my shoulder, I don't think inside my family barrow among the bones of my ancestors is the best place for it," Thorbjorn said.

"Fine. I'm getting up!" I said.

Mjolner meowed again, even more nagging than before. As if it was taking entirely too long for me to pack my pencils and sketchbook back in my bag.

"I wanted to go down there before, and where were you then?" I asked him as I slung the bag over my shoulder.

He just gave me a supercilious look, then disappeared into the tall grass that grew all over the hillside.

I was about to follow him when I turned to look back at Thorbjorn. "I suppose you have to get back out on patrol?" I said resignedly. Another one of our stolen moments, gone too soon.

"No," he said as he got to his feet.

"Wedding errands?" I asked.

"No," he said again, stretching the kinks out of his neck, as if he'd been sitting there for hours. Laying on cold stone certainly had my whole body aching.

But then I realized what he was saying, and why his eyes were smiling at me. "No?" I asked.

"No, I thought I'd see this other fire with you. If it's all right with Mjolner, of course," he said, the last bit pitched loud to carry down the hill.

Mjolner meowed back impatiently. But clearly in the affirmative.

"Let's go then," I said.

I was suddenly feeling much less tired and achy than just a moment before. In fact, I felt like I was filled with sunshine and light.

I was going to need to soak up all of that I could. Because the cold darkness still waited between us and our goal.

CHAPTER SIXTEEN

MJOLNER LED THORBJORN and I through the village to the meadow overlooking Runde and Lake Superior. The cat headed straight for the entrance to the caves below, mostly hidden now by the tall grass, but I wandered instead closer to the top of the bluff so I could look down.

It had been so long since I had been to Runde. It looked the same from up here, tidy little houses mostly concealed under tall pines and beech trees. The roofs of fish houses dotted the rocky shore. A single dirt road wound around from where the bluff almost touched the lake, then up the valley towards me.

I could see the patch of barren ground where my grandmother's Runde cottage had once stood. All the debris left from when the magical tornado had destroyed her home was gone now, but the outline of where the walls had once stood was still clear. Patches of her garden were stubbornly coming back, the fence around it standing as pristine as ever.

Closer still, at the point where the dirt road ended, was the mead hall. Usually this looked like a Viking structure from this side, thatched roof and timber frames that appeared older even than the council hall. But now that the magic was gone from the building, it was permanently in its Runde configuration, a battered-looking meeting hall with a leaky roof and rusted siding.

"Ingrid?" Thorbjorn called from the cave entrance.

"Coming," I said, but still didn't turn away from the view. Now it was the lake itself that held my attention, all steely gray even in the bright light of spring. A few cargo ships were just visible on the horizon, heading towards Michigan and beyond.

Just looking at it gave me a chill. It was not a warm, friendly lake. It was more like my death, waiting for me, cold and deep, a place of unrelenting pressure.

But as I turned away, I thought that was actually comforting. If my death waited for me at the bottom of that lake, it wasn't ahead of me, down in the caves. Funny that should make me feel safe, even safer than knowing Thorbjorn would be by my side.

I hurried to catch up, as Thorbjorn and Mjolner both were well out of sight now. I kept one hand on the stone wall as I ran down the uneven, roughly carved steps that took me down from the sunny meadow to the chill dampness of the cave below.

Thorbjorn and Mjolner were there at the bottom of the stairs, waiting for me. But so was Loke.

"Loke! Is everything all right?" I asked.

"Esja is fine," he said, correctly guessing my chief concern. Then he shrugged. "I was heading into the library at home, and found myself coming out of the cabinet in the back of the storage cave. So, here I am. Apparently where I'm needed."

Thorbjorn frowned at him, and I realized neither Loke nor I had ever explained his magic to anyone save my grandmother.

"Mjolner is leading us down to the deeper fire," I said quickly, deciding now wasn't the time for such a lengthy discussion. "If you're here, he probably wants you along as well."

Mjolner gave a noncommittal meow.

"Is this dangerous?" Thorbjorn asked the cat.

Loke laughed. "Nice to know you think I'm the one to turn to when facing danger."

"I'm not sure why you're here, only that there must be some reason," Thorbjorn grumbled.

"Thanks," Loke said brightly.

"If you're both ready, we should get on with it," I said. They looked at each other and shrugged. Then we all looked at Mjolner.

But Mjolner just sat blinking at Thorbjorn.

"Well, I can certainly get us started," he said after a long moment of silence. He ducked into the storage cave, then came back out with a torch he lit with the sort of lighter used to get gas grills going. Then he lead the way to the far end of the cavern.

I had been through these caves before, twice in the dark, and then that third time with my flashlight. But the torch in Thorbjorn's hand lit up the stone around us in better detail than my handheld flashlight had done. It was easier to see which way to go, and far easier to see which ways not to go. I had followed so many dead-ends before that were clearly visible from the main cave as dead-ends now.

But other details were clearer too. Like the fact that many places that looked like they should be cave openings were blocked off by boulders. Boulders that looked deliberately placed.

"This is where the prisoners are kept?" I asked.

Thorbjorn raised a questioning eyebrow at me.

"When Ingy was here before, her mind was on other things," Loke said from where he strolled behind us, almost lost in the shadows with his head down and his hands deep in his pockets.

"Yes, this is where prisoners are kept," he said. "Not that we have many prisoners. Only those who are a danger to others."

"Like Bera and Halldis," I guessed. Halldis, with her magical powers and penchant for murder, definitely belonged sealed in stone. Bera had also killed a romantic rival, but Bera had no magical gifts on her own.

"Actually, not Bera," Thorbjorn said. "I guess you didn't hear? Bera is in your world now. In a mental health facility where she can get round-the-clock care, but is carefully monitored."

"No, I didn't know that," I said. But it was heartening to hear. I knew that she had been under treatment from a Villmarker woman who had left the Norse village behind to go to a modern university in —as Thorbjorn called it—my world. She had come back to the world of Villmark, if not the village proper, but was still a practicing psychiatrist. "Did Signi arrange it?"

"Yes," Thorbjorn said. "And she is keeping an eye on Bera, in case we need to bring her back. The last thing anyone wants is for her to hurt someone else."

"She never really meant to kill Nefja," I said, but mostly to myself. That was all water under the bridge. "So, who is down here?" I asked instead.

"Currently? Just Halldis," he said, but he spoke in a low voice, barely more than a rumble deep in his chest. Then he pointed to one of the boulders with his torch, a boulder that was far ahead of us at a bend in the cave.

He caught hold of my hand and held it tight, but whether to give me comfort or to keep me from doing something drastic, I wasn't exactly sure. I only held his hand back just as tightly until we had passed that boulder, then gone on around another bend in the cave that was forever spiralling deeper.

"You didn't know where she was?" Loke pondered. "You must have walked past her a couple of times, at least."

"I never sensed her," I admitted. Then, more worrying, "I didn't sense her just now either."

"She's in there," Thorbjorn said with absolute certainty. "She's aware of you the same as you are of her, you know. She can tamp that down like you can. And should've been doing just now."

He gave me a look, but I said nothing. He couldn't tell, one way or the other, and there was no way I was going to admit I had been so distracted just then that I wasn't even sure if I had kept my guard up, or if I'd just let myself glow magic like a luring beacon.

I hoped it was the former. Halldis would be all too delighted by the latter, even if there was nothing she could do currently to take advantage of it. The boulder wasn't the only thing keeping her locked down. My grandmother had worked all manners of bindings on her, I knew. Things she had yet to teach me.

Halldis could occasionally reach me in my dreams, if I wasn't careful. But that was all she had been able to do. Give me a few mild nightmares.

"This is the last turning that I know of," Thorbjorn said as we reached a larger cavern, but one with a lower ceiling above us, and so many stalactites and stalagmites it was only just possible to squirm between them.

I remembered this place from my flashlight trip before. I had spent hours down here, never finding a way deeper in or further down. But I was certain there had to be one.

"You should put the torch out," Loke said. He had been lounging at the cave mouth, watching Thorbjorn with the torch and I with my flashlight conduct an awkward but useless search. "The flashlight too. Mjolner isn't going to take us deeper without it being dark."

"Is that what he told you?" Thorbjorn asked. Not jokingly. We all knew that Mjolner could speak if he wanted to. Even if it was deeply annoying that the person he would actually speak to seemed to be Loke.

"The paths he follows are not for our eyes," Loke said with a shrug.

"Let's get together first," I said before Thorbjorn could stomp out the fire at the end of his torch. I clicked off my flashlight and stuck it back in my bag, then slipped out of the cage of stalactites I had trapped myself in to reach the place where they stood together with Mjolner.

"Ready?" Thorbjorn asked. I seized his free hand, then grasped Loke by the wrist, yanking his hand out of his pocket until I could hold that too. Only then did I nod.

"Ready?" Thorbjorn asked Mjolner.

Mjolner looked around the cavern as if verifying the readiness of everything around us. Then he meowed a bored assent.

Thorbjorn hesitated a heartbeat more, then dropped the torch to the ground and stomped it out under his boot.

We stood together in the inky darkness. It was like, with the sight of fire gone, I could suddenly feel the cold dampness all around us.

Like it was only now seeping into my flesh, digging down into my bones.

I could hear Thorbjorn's even breath on my left, and Loke's slightly quicker breathing on my right. I gave both their hands a squeeze, and they gave an answering squeeze back.

Then, finally, Mjolner meowed softly. He had moved away from us.

"Follow his voice," I whispered to the others, and we all started walking together.

I knew stalactites had been hanging down all around us, low enough for me to hit my head on, let alone Thorbjorn, who had been ducking under the actual cavern ceiling on more than one occasion when we'd been searching the space before. But they were all gone now. There was nothing in front of us but empty, cold darkness. And nothing behind us, I was certain. Or anywhere around us.

I doubted very much we were actually in a cave at all. The ground under my feet still felt like cold, uneven stone, but with my boots on, I couldn't exactly be sure.

Every few shuffling steps, Mjolner would send another guiding meow back our way. It was slow going, and my eyes ached from staring so hard into the blackness that refused to give up any details.

Then suddenly I *could* see something. Mjolner's curve of a tail.

We had reached it. We had reached the deeper ancestral fire. I dropped Thorbjorn and Loke's hands and raced ahead to the light and warmth.

CHAPTER SEVENTEEN

Again, Mjolner did not follow me into the cavern with the fire. He just lingered at the edge of the light in the cave that lead back to the world above. I only noticed this time because Loke started to hover there, too.

"You're here for a reason, remember?" I said as I went back to grab both his hands in mine and pull him after me, into the light of the ancestral fire.

Thorbjorn needed no such urging. He was already standing as close as possible to the flames, staring into them as if he, like Kara and I, could see visions in their sparking dance.

"Thorbjorn?" I said.

"It's nothing," he assured me, but only glanced away from the fire to look at me very briefly before being sucked back into the spectacle of the dancing flames once more. "It *is* different, isn't it? I always felt something when I would guard the other fire, but it was like a shadow compared to this. This is the real thing. How could I ever have thought the other fire was like this?"

"They're related," Loke said. He had let me drag him into the cave, but as soon as I had let him go, he had drifted to the edge of the room and was slouching near the cave mouth, head down and hands in pockets more aggressively than ever.

"That fire was lit from this one," I said to Thorbjorn. "You weren't deceived."

"Maybe," he said doubtfully. "This is where we should stand guard, though."

"My grandmother specifically said the other fire is sacred too," I said. Then I started putting together more bits of things in my head, and they felt true, even if I didn't know them before I heard myself saying them. "That fire is for us to protect, but this fire protects itself. That's why we can't even find it without Mjolner. Only he has the power to approach it."

"This is a gift," Thorbjorn said, holding his palms towards the fire and drinking in the warmth of it.

"I think so, yes," I said. "I don't think we'll ever find it again. Not after we leave this time."

"It's your third time here," Loke said. "That is usually the final number in these sorts of things."

"Then we have to make the most of it," Thorbjorn said, finally turning from the fire to direct his full attention at me. "What do you need to do?"

"Solve the case?" I said uncertainly. But I was already setting my bag on the stone ground, opening it up and taking out all the sketches I had done over the last few days. "I'm certain I have all I need, if I could just *see* it."

"And what do you need from us?" Thorbjorn asked.

That I was less sure about. In all my plans for my return to the ancestral fire, I had assumed I'd be alone. Meditating.

But then things started clicking together in my head again. These rushes of inspiration were almost painful. "I need to draw again, to draw with power. And that has always worked best for me when you were standing over me," I said the last specifically to Thorbjorn.

"What, like, literally?" Loke scoffed, but Thorbjorn just nodded. I sat down with my sketchbook on my knees, charcoal in hand, and he stood behind me. I didn't need to look up, I could just sense that he stood with his hands on the hilts of his weapons. I doubted I would be attacked, certainly not by anything that could be fought with steel, but it was a comfort all the same.

"And me?" Loke asked. I glanced up at him. Anxiety was written all over his features. He didn't like being here, and he was very reluctant to move away from the cave mouth.

He hung around in doorways a lot, I realized. Was it a comfort thing? I didn't think even he was aware of it. But it was like he needed to always be ready to flee in the way only he could.

"I'm going to draw," I said, even as I arranged all of my previous sketches all around me. And his sister's as well. "I'm going to draw again. But not what has happened. I've done enough of that."

"So what, then?" Loke asked.

I could feel Thorbjorn bristling behind me, and could easily picture the scowl he was shooting Loke's way.

But I didn't blame Loke for having questions. Not when I was working so hard to grope at the answers.

"I'm not drawing what happened here before," I said, with more firm confidence now. It was strange, hearing myself speak while I was simultaneously listening to my own words with rapt attention. Because even I didn't know what I was going to say next. "I'm going to draw what has to happen. To connect me to the answers. And I need to borrow some of your power to do it."

"Just like mormor would do," he said with a grim laugh.

"No," I said, "not like mormor. I'm asking for your consent first. I need your power. May I draw from it?"

He opened and closed his mouth twice. But in the end, he just nodded, tucking himself up even tighter against the stone at the cave mouth.

"It won't be much," I promised him. "I think I'm nearly able to do it on my own. But if I'm going to open a door to the past, I need your special power to do it."

"It's not so much a power as a curse," Loke was saying at the same time Thorbjorn objected, "what, now?"

But I heard them both only distantly. Because I had touched charcoal to paper, and the minute that contact had been made, I was lost to the world around me.

I was drawing a woman. Not Yrsa, but a different, older woman. But this woman, too, was dressed as a volva. She even had a staff like my grandmother's, decorated with strips of fur and gleaming beads threaded onto thin strips of leather.

I could see her clearly in my mind. My hand struggled to transcribe all the details I could discern of her face and form, her body language, and the gleam in her eyes. It was like I knew her, only I had not yet met her.

But I was going to.

When I had drawn every detail I could see in my mind's eye, I ended with a circular frame around the image. I had drawn such things before, in my actual works of art. I liked them as borders to illustrations, with details that made them look like living wood, off-shooting branches with leaves and blooms growing from them. And over it all, runes.

The only difference was, back in art school, I had drawn runes I had liked the shape of, or runes that spelled out the names of the gods in the illustration.

This time, I drew each rune as I had learned it. I had so many left to go, but the few I had were enough for this working. Fe. Ur. Thurs. As. Reidh.

Kaun.

Vaguely, distantly, I heard Loke call out.

But I was no longer there.

I was still sitting on the ground by the ancestral fire, but Thorbjorn and Loke were no longer there. Neither was Mjolner.

But Yrsa was. She was before me again, collapsed to the ground with her face turned away from the fire. But her hair was golden, soft and new. The pearls gleamed almost silver-white in the firelight.

And the blood under her was so fresh it filled the air with its pungent copper smell.

I reached out to touch the top of Yrsa's head, but as much as I'd moved back a century, I was still too late. Her body was cold. She had still died alone in this cavern, bleeding out from her head wound.

There was no sign of her attacker. Or attackers.

So why was I here? Why would the magic take me here but no further?

Then I heard footsteps approaching. Soft leather shoes scuffling gently over the dusty stone, occasionally punctuated by the sound of a steel-capped staff striking the ground.

I sat back on my heels, only then realizing that all of my art supplies were gone, left behind in my own time. All I had with me were the clothes on my back. No flashlight, no wand.

And there was nowhere to run. There was only one way out of this cave, and that was the way she was coming in.

She emerged from the darkness of the cave into the firelight, and I saw her again, the woman I had been drawing before. She was dressed as a volva, her gown blue and red trimmed in snowy-white fur. She had a crown braid of silver hair that rivaled Brigida's.

But she also wore a pair of drop earrings, silver and amethyst in a faux-Egyptian design, that jarred with the rest of her image.

"Hello," I said, in my most carefully pronounced Villmarker Norse.

"Hello," she smiled at me, a smile that didn't quite reach her eyes. She was polite, but mistrustful. But then, I'd just appeared out of nowhere from her point of view. So, fair enough.

"I'm Ingrid Torfudottir," I said. "I believe I'm in 1924, in which case perhaps you know my grandmother, Nora Torfudottir?"

The woman took this in without a word. Then she looked around the cavern. The sight of the fire didn't surprise her, so I guessed it was a known place and not a deep secret, at least to her.

Then she looked down at the body on the ground between us. But again, she didn't seem surprised.

"Nora Torfudottir is the name of my granddaughter," the woman said at last. "My name is Ingirun. I am the volva of Villmark." Then she looked down at Yrsa with a frown, as if noticing her outfit for the first time. But as she bent over the body, something flashed golden in the light from the fire, something pinned to her breast.

The cat's head broach with emerald eyes, th one my grandmother had given me. The one that had belonged to her grandmother. This woman.

It took a moment for me to recover from that revelation enough to speak again. "I'm not a volva yet, but I will be one day," I said. "I'm here about this woman, Yrsa."

"Yes, Yrsa," Ingirun said, but then nothing more. I wouldn't want to play poker against this ancestor of mine. She had no tells.

"Did you know she was dead?" I asked.

"No, I did not," she said. She clutched her staff tightly in both her hands, but again gave no other sign of what she was thinking.

"When was the wedding?" I asked.

She looked up at me and blinked slowly. Not exactly an expression of surprise, but that was the emotion I was going with. "Last night," she said.

"Does anyone even realize she is missing?" I asked.

"No. It's just barely dawn," she said. "I woke from a vision dream. I knew she'd be down here. You as well," she added, as if I were a mere afterthought.

"She's cold," I said. "She's been dead for a few hours, anyway. I was hoping to catch whoever did this."

I wanted to gripe about the unreliability of magic, but the words died on my lips. Loke had warned me how tricky his power was, and he was the one most used to practicing it. The fact that I had come so close to my goal was kind of amazing.

But Ingirun was still frowning at me, like she was trying to decide what to do about me. Like I was the bigger problem than the murder victim between us.

"There are three men who are the prime suspects in this death," I said and got to my feet.

"Hold on," she said, shifting to stand with her feet further apart. She looked old, older than my grandmother. But she had that same inner core of spry strength that my grandmother also had. I didn't want to mess with her, not when she had that steel-tipped staff in her hands.

I was pretty sure I was the one who'd be getting hurt in any kind of fight.

"I came here to figure out what happened. I have to see that through," I told her. It was so hard to get the words out, to be sure to pronounce them all clearly. I was too used to switching back to English when I needed to, back in Villmark.

But Ingirun had no problem understanding me. I was pretty sure she was adjusting to my own speech on the fly, mimicking my own flawed accent, not to mock me but to bridge the gap between us. Perhaps she thought it was just a gap in time that made us different. Not that I'd grown up outside our whole culture.

But she was frowning again, that thoughtful frown. "I cast the runes after I woke from my vision," she told me at last, with the air of someone sharing a confidence they aren't sure they should be sharing.

"What did they tell you?" I asked.

"They said I would find you here," she said. "That I can trust you and that I should help you. But that you are dangerous."

"Dangerous?" I had never felt dangerous once in my entire life. Mostly, I was the one *in* danger.

"I can't touch that," she said, pointing down at Yrsa. "And no one can know she is gone until the proper time."

"That makes sense," I said. I had seen enough science fiction movies to know one does not mess with the space/time continuum. If Ingirun buried Yrsa now, she'd not be there when I found the fire. In which case, Ingirun would've never come down to find Yrsa's body.

It was a loop that had to remain a loop.

But there was just one problem with that. "I'm here to find out who did this. How can we do that without anyone knowing that she's here? I mean, you're not the only one who can't touch her, right?"

"You are correct. This must remain undisturbed. Everything must play out as it is meant to. I gather you know already what happens?" she said with a raise of her eyebrows.

"She's not found for a century. It's going to be some time before she's discovered missing, and then she'll be searched for, but not found," I said. "But maybe that's not how the magic works. I mean, in some stories, the people who move through time *can* change things. Maybe we solve this murder now, and I just pop back in my own time..."

But Ingirun was shaking her head at me firmly, raising a hand as if to stop my words.

"No. The runes were very clear. I am to help you this morning, but by midmorning you will be gone," she said. "Now, you have three people you need to meet, correct?"

"The runes told you that?" I asked.

"No, you did," she said. There was just the hint of a smile, a twitch to the corner of her mouth that never quite touched her lips. It reminded me acutely of my own grandmother.

Who was up there, somewhere, in the village Ingirun was about to lead me up to.

"Maybe you should find them and bring them down here?" I suggested.

"No. I understand your fear, and it is a wise one, but I have magic of my own," she said.

"Cloaking us from sight or fogging everyone's memories?" I asked.

This time, the smile stretched all the way across her mouth as she reached out a hand to guide me out of the room. "You know already there was a wedding last night," she told me. "You'd be surprised how little magic it takes to walk unnoticed among those still sleeping off their excesses. Or to fog the memories of the miserably hungover."

"I trust in the old ways," I said, and she laughed.

Then she took me by the arm, struck the floor of the cavern with the steel cap at the end of her staff, and just like that we were standing in the early morning sun in the center of the village commons, the public well behind us and all the party-wrecked square around us.

CHAPTER EIGHTEEN

I WAS sure the tables that ran the length of the public square had been neatly arranged the day before, but they were all askew now. The food had been cleared away, although greasy stains on the once-white tablecloths lingered like ghosts. Tankards for ale were everywhere: laying on their sides on the tabletops, left still half-full standing on the benches, even in kicked-together groupings on the cobblestoned ground.

Some people were sleeping under those tables, or on the benches, or hunched over the tables. But more were sleeping in tents that had been pitched at the north end of the square.

No one was moving. Not at this hour.

"What do we do now?" I asked Ingirun. "Do you know where the three we are looking for are sleeping? If they're even still here."

"We'll talk to them one at a time," she said. She was holding one hand hovering in the air, fingers waggling gently as if she were testing the breeze. Her eyes were half-closed, and she seemed to be murmuring something I couldn't quite hear.

Then I heard a rustle of movement. One of the men who had fallen asleep under a nearby table was sitting up groggily. It took him a moment to fight his way out from under the tablecloth that had already been pulled askew.

But once he was free and stumbled to his feet, I recognized him at once. It was Lodvik. Although seeing him in the flesh, he reminded me less of Thorbjorn than he had in the photograph. He was still tall and broad, but his shuffling walk and the way he seemed to hide behind the locks of his dark hair were all Loke.

"Volva," he said, coming to a halt directly in front of us. Or rather, her. He didn't seem to notice me there at all, but his chagrined demeanor was like a pupil called to the front of the room by a very cross teacher.

"Lodvik," Ingirun said to him reproachfully. Then she glanced over at me. When she spoke next, there was an odd quality to her voice, sort of soft and buzzing. It reminded me of something my grandmother could do, a spell to make her voice heard and heeded by all around her. But this was more like the opposite of that. Like she was speaking for my ears only. "Lodvik is not properly awake now. He will answer my questions honestly, but will remember this only as a dream."

"Can he hear me?" I asked in a low whisper. He still didn't look at me, so I thought the answer would be no.

But Ingirun tipped her head to one side in thought before shrugging. "I think so. But his memories of you will fade all the faster for having nothing in his waking memory to connect them to. He knows me, after all. You, he's never seen before in his life."

"So you should ask the questions, then?" I said.

"I can," she said, then dropped the buzzing effect from her voice to speak to Lodvik. "Lodvik, where is Yrsa?"

"Yrsa?" he said, looking around as if he expected to find her sleeping among the other revelers. "I haven't seen her. Not since..."

But he trailed off, putting a hand over his eyes as if to hide his emotions from us.

"She turned you down," Ingirun said, her voice hard and unsympathetic.

"I knew she would," he admitted. "But I had to speak my heart all the same."

"And now that it is done? What says your heart now?" Ingirun demanded.

"My heart will never speak again," he said, and the hand over his eyes gripped harder, the knuckles white.

"It will," I said, reaching out to touch his arm. But he didn't lower his hand to look at me. "It will take time, but you won't always feel this way."

Ingirun hissed in a breath as if something had caused her sudden pain. I glanced over at her, but she was already in motion, striking my wrist a stinging blow with her staff and then using it to shove me back a step away from Lodvik.

"What was that for?" I asked, shaking my hand vigorously.

"You know what you were doing," she buzzed at me. "You can't change what has already happened."

"*You* know what's going to happen?" I asked.

She gave me an icy look, but whether that meant yes or no, I couldn't guess.

Then she took the buzz out of her voice again to ask Lodvik one last question. "Lodvik, have you done anything that would lead Yrsa to harm?"

He finally dropped the hand from his red-rimmed eyes. The shock on his face was not feigned, I was sure of that. "Yrsa? No. Never!" he said.

"Then you may go back to sleep, and when you wake you will remember none of this," she told him, then shot me a look. As if what I had said was the part that needed to be forgotten the most.

"I was only trying to cheer him up a little," I said, still rubbing at my wrist. Nothing was broken. But that was no accident. That move of hers was far too practiced. I imagined she did it a lot. She knew just how much pressure she could bring to bear without lasting harm.

"If that were all you were trying to do, my magic would not have been screaming in alarm to me," she said. "You cannot change what has already happened. Do not try."

"I understand," I said.

But I didn't. Not really. I just needed those unearthly eyes to focus on something else for a while.

She turned back to the ruins of the party around us. Then she raised her voice again. "Grimmunder. I summon you."

We had to wait longer this time, until I finally heard shuffling foot-steps coming up the road to the west. Apparently, he had gone home at some point in the night, as he seemed to be coming from that house.

He stopped in front of the two of us, but he also only looked at Ingirun. Or looked *around* her; he didn't want to meet her eyes.

"Grimmunder, have you seen Yrsa?" she asked him.

"Yrsa? No, not since I left the party," he said, rubbing at the back of his neck, still mostly talking to her feet. "Were you there so late? I proposed to her, but she said no. So I went home."

"That's all? She turned you down, and you went home to bed? You didn't do anything else?" she asked him pointedly.

"I didn't write any poetry, if that's what you mean," he said glumly. "I don't think I'll ever write again. Not without her to inspire me."

"But you didn't do anything that would harm her?" Ingirun asked.

"No, never," he said. He finally looked up at her, but his eyes were filled with confusion. "Why, where is she?"

"Never mind," Ingirun said with a little wave of her hand. "You can go back home and finish sleeping now."

Grimmunder just nodded, but he still looked confused and uncer-tain about which way he should be walking.

"Grimmunder, the poetry doesn't come from her," I told him. It was like I couldn't help myself. "It comes from within you. She was only one thing in a vast universe of things that can spark the words in your soul."

Grimmunder hesitated. At first I thought this was just his earlier uncertainty overwhelming him. But then he looked up at me. Only for a second, but it was enough. I knew when his eyes met mine that he really saw me standing there. I knew he had heard me.

Then he dropped his eyes again and stumbled away, back towards his house on the west side of the village.

"Did that set off any alarms?" I asked Ingirun. She was already glaring at me, but at my question she just shook her head.

I hoped that was a good sign. If Grimmunder had heard me and heeded my words, maybe he'd still write. Even if everything he'd ever written had burned up with his own body in the fire in the woods, that still felt like a good thing. As lonely as the rest of his life was apparently doomed to be, at least he'd have that outlet left to him.

"Stop grinning," Ingirun growled at me. "Whatever happened, happened. You can't make it happen any more than you could stop it if you tried."

"Sure," I said with a shrug. But I was pretty sure I'd seen more time travel movies than she had. I knew there was at least a chance that the reason things played out the way they did for Grimmunder, it was as likely because I was here to tell him what he needed to hear as for any other reason.

Not everything broke the space/time continuum.

"One last suspect," Ingirun said. But there was a different tone in her voice now. A wary one.

"You saved him for last on purpose?" I guessed.

"Perhaps," she allowed. "Are you ready?"

I nodded. She looked around the square, then called out, "Rolfr. Your volva summons you."

The wait this time was far longer than the first two. I wondered if she should call out again, or if we should go looking, but for some reason I was loath to speak. It was like I didn't want to break that silence. I just kept listening for the sound of anything stirring.

Then finally I heard it: the stomping of heavy boots on the cobble-stoned road to the north. He was coming from the woods, I knew that at once. It was like he brought some of the danger of that place with him, like a cloud trailing behind him.

He wasn't sleeping. Lodvik and Grimmunder had both looked awake as well, their eyes open and seemingly alert. But the minute I saw Rolfr marching up to us, I realized they really had been sleeping the entire time. The difference was so marked.

Ingirun shifted her weight, moving the staff slightly in her hand. It was like a martial artist settling into a fighting stance; she was readying herself for his approach. I stood up straighter too, although what I could do if he decided to attack us, I had no idea.

He stopped in front of us, his eyes moving from Ingirun to me, then back again with a sneer.

"I come because I choose to," he told her.

But he had felt the pull of her magic. Otherwise, why mention it at all?

"You will answer me true," Ingirun said to him. "I will know if you are lying or hiding something from me."

"Who would think they could lie to a volva?" he scoffed. But something flashed through his eyes, a nervousness that was there and gone so quickly I had barely seen it.

He had thought he could lie. But he had changed his mind now that he stood before her. Her gaze *was* unnerving.

"You proposed to Yrsa, and she turned you down," Ingirun said.

Rolfr scoffed even louder than before. "Knew she would."

"Then why do it?" I asked.

He narrowed his eyes at me. "Why not? Third time's the charm, right?"

"That's not a reason," I said, but Ingirun held up her hand, signaling me to silence.

"Rolfr, what have you done this evening since that moment?" she asked. There was another effect on her voice now, still not quite the bell-sound my grandmother used. But to the best of my knowledge, my grandmother had never attempted to command someone to do or say something they didn't want to. And I was pretty sure that was what Ingirun was doing right now with Rolfr.

He was squirming, his calloused fingers rubbing together, his teeth gnashing, his eyes squeezing shut again and again.

"Rolfr, I asked you a question," she said again, with even more magical oomph to her voice.

"You did," he said, quite honestly. "You did. You asked me a question."

"Answer it, Rolfr."

"The other two, so lovesick. Needed to be mocked, didn't they? So up in themselves," he grumbled. "Had to do it. Knew she'd say no, but who cares? Who's she, anyway? Nothing worth troubling over. Nothing at all."

"My question, Rolfr," Ingirun said, kicking up the magical effect on her voice yet another notch.

Rolfr sniffled twice, then dabbed the back of his hand to his suddenly bleeding nose.

"Answer the question," I begged him.

He looked up at me as if he'd forgotten I was even there, like he was startled to see me. "I didn't do a thing," he said. All the scorn was gone from his voice, and his blue eyes were clear and earnest. "I went into the forest to patrol. I needed to keep moving, to do something that wasn't completely meaningless. Like this whole wedding party. So meaningless."

"And Yrsa?" Ingirun asked, still at full boom with the magic.

Rolfr flinched, then pressed a sleeve to his nose as a fresh burst of blood dripped down. "I didn't see her after. Why would I? I promise you, she's nothing to me. I only proposed because Lodvik and Grimmunder were both *so* self-important with it. The whole party was disgusting. All of you are. It's all so fake."

"Very well, Rolfr. You may go," Ingirun said, finally back in her normal voice.

"Wait!" I said, catching at her arm. She glared down at my hand and I let her go at once before I got my wrist rapped again. "Isn't there something we can do? In the Villmark of my time, there is a psychiatrist. Is there anyone like that here? Someone he can talk to? There's clearly something not right with him."

"No, we have nothing like that here," she said. She turned back to Rolfr, who was still hovering uncertainly before us. "You may go."

He nodded and turned back towards the north, towards the forest. He marched back up the road, his boots ringing loudly.

I bit at my lip. He raised so many red flags in my mind, I couldn't stand to see him walk away without warning everyone who would likely come into contact with him again.

But Ingirun rested a hand on my arm, even giving it a sympathetic squeeze. "I've seen into Rolfr's heart. Ever since he was a young boy. Nothing I've tried has been any help to him. But you and I both know his fate. He will be stopped before he is a danger. That is the best we can hope for."

I nodded. I knew she was right, but I still didn't like it.

"So that's your three suspects, none of them guilty," she said. There was a hint of a question in her voice.

"No, I don't think they are," I admitted.

"So what would you like to do now?" she asked me.

I pondered, but only briefly. I already knew, in my heart.

"I need to go back to the fire," I said.

And in a flash, we were there.

CHAPTER NINETEEN

WE WERE BACK in the old familiar cave, once more standing over Yrsa's body. But no closer to understanding just what had happened to her.

"How did she even get down here?" I asked, exasperated.

"I'm not sure any other question matters as much as that one," Ingirun said. She knelt by Yrsa's side, touching the hair at the side of her face, away from the bloody injury.

"I've not found an entrance to this cave I can walk through," I said. "Each time, my cat has led me here. He's a special cat."

"He must be," Ingirun said, unsurprised.

"How do you do that thing…?" I asked, trying to mimic the gesture she used with her staff to teleport us out and back again.

"It only brings me to this fire and back," she said. "And now that I've been here three times, it will never work for me again. When I leave this cave this time, I'll never be back."

"So that *is* a rule?" I asked. Then I counted back. "This is my fourth time here."

"Three in your own time, an extra in the past," Ingirun guessed, and I nodded. "Also, this fourth time is more my doing than yours.

Yes, I think you'll find when you return to your own time, this place will be lost to you forever."

"But why?"

"The older fire is a tricky thing, and not to be treated lightly," Ingirun said grimly. But then she laughed, a harsh, self-mocking sound. "And here I thought my final visits to this cave would be so portentous. I saved them up my whole, long life."

"Sorry?" I said, not sure she even wanted my apology. But I had taken up her last two visits to the fire, and it was starting to look like the whole thing had been pointless.

"Don't be," she said with a little wave of her hand. "I came here for the first time when I was far too young for such things. To have it well and truly over now is a bit of a relief. It can't call me again. There's a freedom in that."

"What happened that first time?" I asked.

But she just shook her head at me. "I won't tell that tale here, not where the flames are always listening. I'll only say, if your three times are up too, it's just as well. The other fire, the one behind the waterfall near the village, is far better for volva magic than this monstrosity."

I looked at the fire nervously. *She* was the one who said it was listening, and yet she made free with the insults.

"I used the power from this fire to get here," I said. "I don't think I could've done the same from the other fire."

"Likely not," Ingirun said. "It doesn't have the same power, but what power it does have is far more reliable. It won't turn away from you. Or worse, turn against you. They'll work with you. Not like these flames. These flames resist any magic of control."

She pulled her cloak closer around herself, as if feeling a sudden chill. Which was impossible; the two of us were standing very near that bonfire. But I supposed she was remembering again her earlier visit, the one she wasn't speaking of.

"Do you know why there are two?" I asked her.

She gave me a surprised look. "I thought that was known to all volvas. The second, safer fire was crafted for our use by Torfa's granddaughter. She could not bring herself to destroy this one, but she *could* hide it, and try to protect the rest of us from its wilder ways."

"Granddaughter," I said, lost in thought. Then I looked over at the woman beside me. My grandmother's grandmother.

"I see you're working it out," she said with a sad smile. "Yes, all of us that descend from Torfa call ourselves Torfudottirs, but the power waxes and wanes. It's usually stronger every other generation. Not always, but usually. Torfa's own daughter only did rudimentary magic, but *her* daughter is the closest we ever came to having a volva as powerful as Torfa herself had been."

"And your daughter?" I asked.

The smile grew sadder still. "She knows enough to teach her daughter the basics. But it was clear when she was young that she would never have the calling to truly pursue the knowledge. Just as it's been clear since she was very young that my granddaughter *does* have that calling."

"It's kind of sad, isn't it?" I asked.

She didn't answer right away, just gazed into the flames as if lost in memories. Then she said, "I think it's necessary, perhaps. If every generation had the same drive to master our craft, I fear we'd stop having babies. And then where would our community be? Every other generation focusing on other things, it's enough to keep us going."

"But not all users of magic are Torfudottirs, or even volvas," I said.

"That is true," she said, turning to look down at Yrsa again. "But this is Torfa's fire. That is a very particular sort of magic. It should only be her descendants who can reach this place. You see what I'm saying? The bigger mystery that needs to be solved isn't who killed Yrsa, but how she arrived here at all. Not having that answer puts us all in grave danger."

"Why?" I asked. Because it felt like she meant something more specific than I was grasping.

"The spells that hide Villmark from the wider world are based around this fire, not the other one," Ingirun said. "Without those spells, we'd be naked and vulnerable."

"The wider world isn't so bad," I said. I gestured towards her own earrings, their art deco design was definitely not from Villmark. "It has a lot to recommend it."

"Mingling with the wider world is not the danger," Ingirun said, again giving me that flabbergasted look, like she couldn't believe she had to explain this to me. "There is something out there that was hunting us. That's why we left Old Norway, why Torfa brought us here, and why she hid us."

"But that was centuries ago," I said.

"You know as well as I do that to some things that is a mere blink of an eye," she said. "This fire must be protected."

I looked down at Yrsa. I knew what Ingirun said was right, that protecting the fire was a bigger priority than solving Yrsa's murder.

But I was still sure that doing one would handle the other.

Only I had nothing with me to even work with anymore. I patted my pockets, but everything I had brought into the cave was back in my own time, with Loke and Thorbjorn. My art supplies, my bag, my flashlight and wand. Even the sketchbook and charcoal I had been holding were gone.

"What do you need?" Ingirun asked.

"Something to draw with," I said. "That's how my magic works. I can draw what happened to Yrsa. Maybe being here, closer to her death, I'll get better images than I did in my time. Only I left all my supplies behind in my time, and I guess if you go, you'll never get back here again."

"No, that's true," Ingirun said, looking around the cave as if I'd somehow missed seeing paper and implements in a shadowy corner.

Then she opened a soft fur bag that hung from her belt. She dug through it. I couldn't see what was going on behind the lifted flap, but smells of crushed herbs tickled my nose as she crinkled things together.

"Here," she said at last, thrusting two things into my hands. One was a stub of a pencil, like the kind you keep score with when bowling or playing miniature golf. The other was a copy of the pulp magazine *Weird Tales*.

"Earrings aren't the only thing I like about the wider world," she said, her cheeks flushing ever so slightly pink.

"Of course," I said, flipping through the book. It was strange. I had seen magazines like this before, but always in a battered, faded, yellowed condition. This one was still cheaply made, of course, but it was also new. I could smell the freshness of the ink and paper.

"Just avoid the H.P. Lovecraft story if you can," Ingirun grumbled. "I haven't read that one yet."

I flipped to the table of contents and saw the story she was referring to was "The Rats in the Walls."

"It's a good one," I assured her, then picked another section of the magazine. It was a story by no one whose name was still known in my day. It also featured a lot of dialogue, and hence a lot of white space.

I tuned out the words, put the pencil to the page, and started to draw.

CHAPTER TWENTY

WHEN I SAT BACK with a blink some time later, I had drawn a sacrifice scene again. Kauns were everywhere in the margins, but the central image was much clearer. Perhaps it was the hard graphite of the pencil rather than the soft darkness of charcoal that made the difference. But mostly I think it was being closer to the time of death that gave me more images to work with.

Interesting. Time *did* matter.

"Look," I said, catching Ingirun's attention. She had been pacing on the far side of the fire, trying not to disturb me as I worked, but she came back to my side to peer over my shoulder. "There is Yrsa, on her knees. But these two figures behind her aren't men at all. Do you know them?"

Ingirun took the magazine from me to get a better look. The two women were clearly sketched, one old and one young. They both looked familiar to me, but that was because they both looked like Halldis. Halldis, who could make herself look younger through her magic, but was far older than she seemed.

When I was in the north, I had met another woman who had looked a lot like Halldis and these two women. It wasn't just in the way they dressed provocatively or arranged their golden locks of hair.

It was in their body language and even the features of their face. It was like they were all sister-clones from the same source, only generation after generation of them.

"I don't know them, but I've seen women like this before," Ingirun said grimly. "They are trouble. Usually this is just trouble with the patrols. But occasionally they come into the village and cause trouble here."

"My grandmother had a woman like this who wanted to be her apprentice, before I came home," I said. Ingirun gave me a confused look, and I had to back up. "I grew up outside of Villmark. My mother didn't feel the calling to be a volva, so she followed my father to a different city and I grew up there. I only came home less than a year ago. I've been working to catch up ever since."

I could feel my cheeks burning, admitting that I wasn't as practiced a volva as I'd probably led her to believe.

But she just looked at me with deep respect. Then she asked, "What happened to this woman? This apprentice?"

"She is imprisoned in the caves above this place," I said.

Ingirun touched the back of her hand to her mouth, a quick, spontaneous gesture of shock. "I'm not sure that's safe."

"I'm not so sure myself, anymore," I agreed.

"We need to know more about what happened in this scene," Ingirun said.

"I can try drawing again," I offered, reaching for the magazine, but she held it away from me.

"No, I have a different idea. Sit with me here."

I sat beside her on the stone cave floor, closer to the bonfire than was really comfortable. She spread the magazine out on the floor between us. Then she took something from her bag, one of the bundles of herbs I had smelled before, and tossed it into the fire.

I started to cough and choke at once. The smoke was very noxious and seemed to be floating right at us in a thick cloud. Ingirun grabbed my wrist and held me there when I started to get up to run for clearer air.

Then, it was like something in my head just clicked. I stopped coughing and breathed deeply, taking in great lungfuls of air so oxygen-rich it made me dizzy.

I nearly jumped at the sound of someone's cries echoing through the caves, but Ingirun's hand still held me fast. I had to pivot in place to see the cave mouth.

Yrsa came in, her pearls swinging as she walked with her head bent forward. She wasn't bleeding yet, but I suspected from the way she was stumbling about that she had been hit on the head at least once already. She was crying and pleading, her words in a thick rush my brain couldn't parse into meaning. Like it wasn't even Villmarker Norse, but something else.

Then two women behind her came into view, and my blood ran cold. It was one thing to see it in a sketch, quite another more unsettling thing to see it in real life, up close. Both of them so eerily familiar, although I had never met them before. Both of them looking like they could be sisters to each other, and sisters to the women I had known. Same long blonde hair that hung in heavy curls and tendrils down their backs, so thick and yet it moved as they walked, like it was a living thing. Same eyes the shade of green that brought to mind snakes and poison.

Sisters who were decades apart in age, but still, sisters.

Like Halldis, the woman who longed to be my grandmother's apprentice, had looked like both of them. Hulda, who I had met in the north, had looked like them.

The woman who hadn't felt human that had taken the Thors under her power far in the north looked like them.

But neither of the two women I was looking at now were any of those three. I was looking at two more specimens of the same sisterly clan of witches who were not volvas.

The older gave Yrsa's shoulder a shove, hard enough to send her to her knees. But she caught herself before she could tumble into the roaring fire, turning to look back over her shoulder at the two of them.

They towered over Yrsa, and I realized this was another aspect of the same sort of glamor magic that Halldis had used to make herself young and beautiful. They were using it to make themselves tall and imperious.

And it was working. Yrsa was trembling close to the ground, and I wanted to pull away as well. I wanted to flee from the cold, angry beauty of their ethereal faces.

It was like they weren't even trying to look human anymore.

But I didn't know what else they could be.

I looked over at Ingirun, but she was engrossed in the scene before us. Not preoccupied with the two women the way I was, more curious to see what would happen next.

Not that we didn't already know.

But Yrsa was pleading again, only this time I could understand her.

"You had your chance," the older woman snapped at her. "You refused us. All over a vision. Don't you know visions lie?"

"Visions lie, Yrsa," the younger woman said in a soft hiss of a voice. "Visions lie."

"Or," the older woman said brightly, lifting a finger as if she were a lawyer making a point that was only a technicality, really. "Or powerful forces contrive to make the visions true."

"Like now," the younger woman said with a grin. She moved around Yrsa, contorting her body in a snaky way, bending to look into Yrsa's face. "This is what you saw in your vision, wasn't it? You, here, in the most forbidden of places—"

"The most sacred of places," Yrsa interrupted, lifting her chin defiantly.

The younger woman looked up at the older woman, who just lifted her hands as if weighing two objects and finding them the same.

"As you like it," the younger woman said to Yrsa with a sneer. "The point is, you wouldn't even be here if you'd just come to us like you swore to."

"I wasn't sworn yet," Yrsa said. The younger woman snapped close to her face, again like a snake, and Yrsa collapsed in on herself, hugging her arms tightly around her as she trembled, all defiance gone.

"You were sworn to be sworn," the older woman said. "There was no backing out. You had already come too far."

"And now the very nightmare that kept you away from us is coming to pass," the younger woman said, still circling and stooping over Yrsa. "Don't you wonder how we can stand it? Isn't your sacred flame supposed to be death to us? And yet, all I feel is warmth."

She stretched out her hands to the fire, even rubbing them together to make her point.

"Enough," the older woman said. "She has refused us. We don't bond with sisters who refuse us."

"But we don't let them walk away, either," the younger woman said. She turned away from the fire, squatting in front of Yrsa. Yrsa looked up at her, and it was like she was trapped by those eyes. Her trembling stopped, and her arms fell to her sides. She just knelt there, staring at the younger woman.

I was caught up in the moment as well, so much so I didn't realize the older woman had stepped up behind with a rock in her hand until I heard the crack of it against Yrsa's skull.

Then Yrsa slumped forward, soundlessly, falling into the posture I had grown to know so well.

The older woman tossed the rock into the heart of the fire, then dusted off her hands.

"There's that dealt with," she said. But then she frowned. "Not how I saw this going."

"She was supposed to be one of us," the younger woman said as she got to her feet, carefully stepping back so the blood flowing from Yrsa's head didn't touch the toes of her slippers.

"It was never a sure thing," the older woman said. But then she made an angry growling sound of pure frustration. "Well, it's over now. Back to the north for me. What about you?"

"Back to my village," the younger woman said, smoothing her hand over her belly. "I have months to go, but I like being home before they're born, you know?"

"I know," the older woman said with a smile. "Bond with her tightly. There are so few of us left."

Then the vision wavered. The smoke from the fire was suddenly thicker again, the smell cloying. This time, when I stumbled away to find fresher air, Ingirun followed me.

After a few minutes in the dark cave at about the point where Mjolner would come no closer, we got our breath back.

"What are they?" I asked her. Because there was no doubt in my mind that they weren't human.

"I don't know," she admitted. "But they have left Villmark for now. I don't think they will be back in my lifetime. But I fear they will in yours."

"*I* fear they already have," I said.

"They are looking to make sisters," Ingirun said. "Not all who look like them are... whatever they are. Some *are* human."

"Will you send patrols out to find them?" I asked. "One was going far to the north, but the other was going to one of the villages that is closer. I think I might even know which one."

But Ingirun was already shaking her head. "No, this mystery is not for my time to solve. The rune casting that drew me here was very clear on that point. I can assist you, but once I leave this cave, it will be as if all of this is forgotten by me. I can't do a thing. It's already happened."

I nodded, not wanting to argue the point. But I felt bad for Yrsa. She had gotten caught up in something she should've known better than to mess with, but by the time she grew wise to it, it was too late. She was in too deep.

But she was so young.

"Yrsa's remains are already with her sister's descendants," I said.

Ingirun raised her eyebrows at the word "sister" but said nothing.

"Justice might be trickier," I added.

"No one in Villmark owes a blood price," she said. "This was no crime, then. Only a random bit of bad luck. Like a bear attack."

"Maybe," I said. But I knew I didn't believe that. Bears had no malice, only fear or occasionally natural aggression.

But those two women, whatever they really were, their hearts were full of malice. It radiated out of their bodies like heat. It blazed out of their eyes.

"I wish you the best of luck, granddaughter's granddaughter," Ingirun said, putting a hand on my shoulder.

"Thank you," I said. But then I was forced to admit, "I'm not exactly sure how I'm going to get home again. I drew myself here, but I was sort of borrowing someone else's power at the same time."

"I think you'll find putting things back the way they are meant to be is always easier magic than taking such an excessively unnatural action as moving through time," she said.

I remembered the magazine she kept with her magic supplies. *Weird Tales*. 1924 might be a little early for time travel fiction, but, then again, she might know more than I thought she did about science fictional things.

"Should I try meditating?" I asked her.

But she just smiled at me. "I think we'll see if it isn't a great deal easier than that."

I had no idea what she was talking about. But then she rapped the steel cap of her staff on the stone floor, one quick snap of noise.

Then she was gone, or I was. Or, I suppose, we both were.

All I knew was that when I opened my eyes, I was flat on my back, staring up at the dancing patterns of shadow and firelight on the stalactites hanging down from the cavern ceiling.

CHAPTER TWENTY-ONE

I ONLY HAD a moment to enjoy the rest and the light show before two concerned faces loomed over me, blocking the view.

"I'm all right," I said, but didn't fight the hands that helped me sit up. It was like I had just slumped over. My legs were still more or less crossed, my sketchbook tipped off my knees but not quite sprawled on the floor. "How long was I out?"

"Out?" Thorbjorn said, confused.

"You just gasped, like you were sucking in air after deep diving, and then you fell over backwards," Loke told me. "How long do *you* think you were out?"

"Most of a day," I said, pressing a hand to my forehead. "I guess I'm not quite synced back up from my first trip down here when I lost a bunch of days."

"I don't like this fire," Thorbjorn said, but low, as if he were afraid the fire would overhear him.

"I've been warned that its power is not to be trusted," I told him.

"By who?" Loke asked.

"Ingirun. My grandmother's grandmother," I said. Then I sucked in a deep breath. My brain felt like it needed the extra oxygen, but when that look of concern rushed back to both of their faces, I regretted the impulse. "I know who killed Yrsa."

"You drew it?" Loke said, picking up the sketchbook.

"Yes, but not in there. I went back into the past, questioned all the suspects, then did another drawing session with Ingirun there with me," I said. "The murderer wasn't anyone from Villmark."

"So the case is closed, as they say?" Loke asked.

"No. Far from it," I said as I got to my feet. "We need to get back up to the caves where we keep the prisoners."

"Halldis did it?" Loke asked.

"No, but she's definitely involved," I said. I picked up my scattered art supplies and shoved them all back into the bag, then slung the bag over my shoulder. "Mjolner, are you ready to take us back?"

"Don't you need council permission to talk to Halldis?" Loke asked.

"You're going to hassle me about getting permission first?" I asked him.

"Not me, no. It's just, if it were me, and I were looking to do a little rule breaking, I wouldn't have brought the big guy," he said, cocking a thumb over his shoulder at Thorbjorn standing over us both.

"The big guy can hear you," Thorbjorn grumbled. But then he grabbed my elbow and said earnestly, "If time is not of the essence, you *should* speak to the council first."

"Told you," Loke snickered.

"Time is not of the essence," I admitted. Yrsa was a century dead, her murderers long gone. And while they were still a danger, or at least their clan or whatever was a danger, it wasn't an imminent one.

And yet.

"What is it, then?" Thorbjorn asked me.

"I need to change my relationship with the council," I said. "I know I'm not my grandmother, not even close. But the time is past for their opinions to outweigh my own on what is safe and what is a risk for how I use my power. Some things are my discretion as a volva, and they are going to have to adjust."

"Is now the time for that?" Thorbjorn asked.

I could feel Loke's eyes on me, could sense the smirk he was deep enough in the shadows away from the fire to hide from me. But I tuned him out.

I knew I was right.

"I've been to this fire four times now," I said, holding out a single hand towards the warmth of its flames. "The normal limit is three."

"That changes things?" Thorbjorn asked.

"Of course it does," Loke said, and stepped out of the shadows to loop his arm through mine. "And it's past time for us to get away from it. I don't like this fire either."

"Let's go, then," I said, and caught hold of Thorbjorn's arm with my free hand. Then we walked together down the narrowing cave to where Mjolner sat waiting for us.

But before the cave turned, I looked back one last time.

I hadn't tried to communicate with Torfa. Haraldr had warned me not to. I agreed with him that I wasn't remotely ready. And yet, without understanding the rules, I had used up all my chances to meditate at her own magical fire.

Was that a mistake I was going to regret?

No, I decided. Torfa *was* Villmark. Her power still kept it safe. The fire was just a part of that. In the future, if I needed to find her, I was certain I would find a way to get to her.

Somehow.

Mjolner led us back through the cold dark, then stopped at the exact point where Thorbjorn had dropped the torch. I flicked on my flashlight, but the warmth of the torchlight when he got it lit was far preferable to the dim chill of the electric bulb.

Mjolner was still leading the way, back up through the long spiralling cave. But he stopped outside of Halldis' stone-blocked cave and turned to look at me.

"See? He knows," I said.

"And he has proven his worth, battling these strange women," Thorbjorn said seriously. "He has protected you from them on more than one occasion."

"That's true," I said. But I didn't really like relying on that. It was too much like thrusting my own cat into danger for my sake. It didn't quite feel right.

"Wait, what are we talking about?" Loke asked.

"Mjolner and I are going through the wall," I said, then glanced up at Thorbjorn. He nodded; that was what he had been thinking as well. I looked back at Loke. "It's safer than rolling back the stone. You and Thorbjorn will wait here until we come back out."

"I can just open a door," Loke said.

"No, I don't want you doing that," I said. "There's a good chance Halldis doesn't know about your power. And if she doesn't, I would prefer to keep it that way. But look, I'm only doing this now because I'll have two men out here who can come in and get me if I run into trouble in there. You're my backup."

"You like this idea?" Loke asked Thorbjorn, almost accusingly.

"I think arguing against it will end up being quite futile," Thorbjorn said with a shrug.

I suspected I was the one smirking now, and I struggled to keep my expression serious.

"Fine," Loke said, throwing up his hands. "We'll wait out here in the hall. But this better be a short conversation."

"I have a feeling she's not going to want to tell me anything useful at all, but I want to sound her out," I said. I unslung my art bag and set it on the floor, but kept my wand tucked in my belt. Then I looked down at Mjolner. "Ready?"

He gave me a slow blink of his yellowish-green eyes.

I blinked back, involuntarily, as if it were contagious, like a yawn. It was a slow blink as well, and when my eyes opened again, I was in shadowy darkness.

Mjolner meowed up at me. Then my eyes adjusted. I was at the top of a narrow tunnel. It wasn't a natural rock formation, more like something dug by a stone-eating worm. It spiraled down away from the stone blocking the way out behind me. Whatever lay at the bottom was beyond at least one turning of the passage, but I could see light flickering up at me.

I walked down the tunnel, Mjolner keeping pace beside me. But before the bottom was even in view, a voice called up to me.

"Well met, Ingrid Torfudottir. I was beginning to despair of us ever meeting again."

It was Halldis. She sounded the same as ever. Prison life, even in a prison such as this where she was confined to a single cave with no hope of sunlight or moonlight ever, hadn't changed her.

Then I reached the last turning in the tunnel and saw the squared-off space that was her entire world now. There was a table against the wall at the bottom of the tunnel, a table set with two chairs, as if in case she had company.

Then I saw a bookshelf stuffed with books, all modern novels, without a hint of a spell book anywhere among them. A dark red overstuffed chair was arranged beside it, with a currently unlit reading lamp positioned to cast light down on the lap of whoever was sitting in that chair.

She had a bed piled high with wool blankets and furs, but more furs spread across the stone floor instead of carpeting, all the way up to the base of the tunnel.

And a fireplace took up the entire back wall, large enough for any of the Thors to lie down in comfortably. It was filled with logs that were in a full crackling blaze of heat and light. There was no woodbox nearby to replenish it, and I suspected magic was at play. But it was very effective at making the space not just warm but also dry.

Like we weren't in a cave at all.

"It's not as comfortable as you'd think, once you've been here more than a few hours," Halldis said as if reading my mind. Then I finally saw her, sitting on a stool next to a screened-off corner. I could just see the clawed feet of a massive bathtub beyond the wooden screen. She was barefoot, wearing nothing but a shift, and the hair she was combing was damp still.

I had just missed interrupting her in the bath.

"He can stay outside my cave if you want to have any conversation with me at all," she said with sudden venom. I turned to look at Mjolner, who had hesitated with a single six-toed paw hovering over the fur-strewn floor. He pulled the paw back and sat at the very edge of the tunnel, bathing himself blithely as if that had been what he had been planning to do in the first place.

"You all really hate my cat, don't you?" I said, almost amused.

Almost.

She just gave me a shaded look. "I am not a 'you all'."

"No, but you're part of one," I said. I wandered over to the bookshelf and scanned the spines. "Who brings the books?" I asked her.

"If you don't know, I don't think I should be the one to tell you," she said.

"Signi, then," I guessed.

She said nothing, just carried on combing out her thick locks of golden hair.

I risked giving her a more thorough looking over. She was as gorgeous as ever, even dressed simply as she was. I was sure if she got up from that stool and walked over to me, she could work a slinky strut that would put Ann-Margret to shame.

Funny she could still draw power for that. I could feel how the structure of this place was wicking away magic. It was making me feel strangely exhausted after only a few minutes inside.

But she could still summon power, despite those constraints.

And vanity was what she chose to spend that power on. Even though no one ever came down to see her.

I took out my wand and waved it before my eyes. For just an instant, I saw a vision of her as she truly was: a crone. A remarkably well-preserved crone, but still.

But the instant she saw my wand, she lunged for it, crossing the room in a burst of speed I hadn't seen coming. I stepped one foot back, but only to get into something more like a fighting stance.

And when I leveled the wand at her, she stopped.

"What are you?" I demanded.

"You know what I am," she sneered at me. "Just a woman, a woman who devoted her life to the same knowledge, the same craft as you pursue now. A woman who was rejected, not worthy of the greater mysteries. In the eyes of your grandmother."

"But someone else taught you," I said.

"Taught me what, my dear little volva?" she asked in feigned innocence. "What do I know that I couldn't glean from books? Poisons? Illusions? Glamor?" She said the last word with the smallest oomph of magic, striking a pose and flaring up her power so high it almost hurt to look at her.

She was, for a flash, indescribably beautiful. My artist self wanted to capture that beauty, but my usual techniques wouldn't be enough. I'd need to break out oil paints. Or perhaps sculpture...

Halldis's laugh pulled me out of my reverie. I realized my wand had drooped, and I raised it to point it at her again. But she didn't look remotely threatened.

"I will find out what is happening out there, and I will find out what your place in everything is," I said to her.

"I'm sure you will," she said, batting her eyes at me.

Mjolner gave a meow, for all the world like a prison guard telling me visiting hours were over. I gave him a nod and tucked my wand away. I was going to leave Halldis without another word, but she wasn't going to let it go like that.

"I'm sure you will, my dear little volva," she called after me as I climbed the tunnel back up to the cave. "But will you do it in time? That's the question, Ingrid Torfudottir. That is always the question."

I said nothing, but I didn't need to.

We both knew she was right.

CHAPTER TWENTY-TWO

I HAD TRIPPED SOMETHING, going into Halldis's cell. There was no other explanation for how everyone knew I'd been in there before we had even gotten back out of the caves.

The entire council met us in the meadow overlooking Lake Superior.

The entire council, plus my grandmother.

They relented, a little, when Thorbjorn told them he had been watching over me the whole time.

But mostly it was the cold wind off the lake and the hint of rain in the air that got everyone calmed down enough to adjourn to the council hall.

At some point during the walk into town, we lost Loke. I didn't see it happen. One minute he was there, and the next he wasn't. But that was usual for him. And he had played his part. I doubted the others had even noticed he was there when Mjolner, Thorbjorn, and I had come out of the deeper caves.

As much as I was sure it was some sort of monitoring spell my grandmother had put on Halldis's cell that had told her I had gone in there, how Vali knew I had solved the case was beyond me. I hadn't even mentioned it yet to the council, wanting to get in out of the rain before the light sprinkles we were walking through became the downpour I sensed approaching.

But he was there, at the top of the stairs, when we reached the doors. And the look on his face told me everything.

He not only knew I knew, he knew it was no one in Villmark.

His expression was relieved but tormented at the same time. That curse he had nursed throughout his life was going to be no use in the end. I didn't want to think about what he'd given up, choosing to focus on that instead.

Only his entire life.

We all went into the hall just as the rain picked up. I could hear it drumming on the thatched roof over our heads, but the braziers were burning bright and warm, and the space below that roof was cozy.

The council climbed the dais to take their places on the three-legged stools. Thorbjorn stood off to one side, more observer than participant. Vali was also off to the side, but closer, like he wanted to be ready to rush in if the moment required it.

My grandmother and I took our customary places before the council, but I didn't kneel. And neither did she. Not a word had passed between us, not even a look. And yet we were on the exact same page.

The most surprising thing about that was how unsurprised I felt about it. It was like I had already known she'd reached the same conclusion about our role versus the council as I had. Was that just because she knew I had spoken to Halldis alone? Did that moment make as large a change in her mind as it did in mine?

But that wasn't something I wanted to discuss with her in front of the council. That would have to wait.

"Start from the beginning," my grandmother said to me, and Brigida gestured towards me as if invoking me to speak.

"Nothing I could do here and now was helpful in eliminating any of the three suspects," I said. "They all had a possible motive, having been turned down after making marriage proposals, but there was no evidence of any of them being near Yrsa after that.

"So I went back to the scene of the crime. The older ancestral fire. The original one, imbued with magic by Torfa herself," I said.

And how much more did I have to tell my grandmother about that? It was overwhelming. I wished I could've talked to her first, and the council second.

But she just nodded at me to continue.

"I used that fire to go back to the time of the wedding, the last time Yrsa was seen," I said. "I questioned each of the suspects again, this time with the aid of the volva from that time. She had the power to compel them to answer and forbid them to lie. They each spoke true. None of them were the killer."

"You were actually there, or this was a vision?" Brigida asked, confused.

"All that matters are the answers she came back with," my grandmother said. She wasn't looking at me, but there was no doubt from her firm tone that she was pretty much commanding the three of them not to ask me more about it.

My grandmother had been searching for a possible source of magic that Vali could use to lay a curse. Had she found something? Something so large it was making her behave this way? Or was it truly just my decision to see Halldis?

"What can you tell us?" Valki asked me with an exaggerated show of patience.

"Yrsa was being lured away by women from a nearby village," I said. "They were deceiving her, telling her they were volvas and could make her a volva as well." I was assuming a lot, based on Yrsa's outfit, but it felt right when I said it out loud. It fit. "She must have had some power of her own, because she had a dream or vision that told her these women were not to be trusted. But it was too late. They couldn't let her back out. She knew too much. So they took her to the hidden place where Torfa's fire still burns, and they killed her there. Then they fled, one back to their village, the other far to the north."

"What village?" Valki asked, resting a hand on the hilt of the knife in his belt.

"They didn't say a name, but I believe it is the one that Nilda went to last month, in search of the woman named Hulda," I said.

"She is part of this?" Haraldr asked. "And the other woman who went further north? That is the other woman you told us about, the one who could control the Maras?"

"No, they weren't the same women," I said.

"It was a century ago," Brigida said to Haraldr.

"More than that, I saw their faces in a vision. They are definitely not the same individuals," I said. "But I think they are part of some larger group, one that has been trying to worm its way into Villmark for some time now."

"That's why you went to see Halldis," Valki guessed.

"Yes. She's part of it," I said.

"And what did you learn from her?" he asked.

I chewed at my lip. I had a lot of strong impressions from my time in her cell, but I hadn't had a moment alone to go over any of it in my own mind. I would've loved an hour or two at my drawing table to really work it out.

"First impressions," my grandmother suggested.

"She is still drawing magic," I said. "She is altering her appearance, and she can move with unearthly speed when she wants to."

"You put wards--" Brigida started to say.

"All that I knew," my grandmother said, interrupting her. "The entire room should be sealed. I don't know where she could be pulling from."

"It needs to be looked into," Haraldr said with a frown. His hands twitched like he longed to reach for his books straight away.

"I trust Nilda when she tells me the village was abandoned, but I think I need to see it with my own eyes," I said.

"Not alone," Thorbjorn said, but not to me. To the council.

"It's all part of the larger mystery," Valki said with a sigh. "The artifacts, the darkness Ingrid speaks of. All of it."

"These women who murdered my sister, they just fled?" Vali asked.

I had almost forgotten he was still there. But I turned to him now to say, "I believe they were acting under orders from someone... well, some*thing*, really, that is still unknown to me."

"To us," my grandmother corrected me.

"But they were not a member of any family who lies under the dominion of this council," Vali went on. "No one I can demand a blood price from."

"No, I'm afraid not," I said.

"But her bones have been laid to rest," my grandmother said to him. "And the mystery of her death is solved. Her ghost will rest easy now. What of you?"

Vali shifted his weight from foot to foot. The week of moving around, demanding things of me and the council, were taking a visible toll on him. The hands that he was clenching tightly together were still shaking terribly.

Finally, he looked up at me with those milky eyes that never seemed to quite see me, and he said, "I am satisfied. Thank you, Ingrid Torfudottir. I think I will go home now. Go home and rest."

"I will walk with you," Thorbjorn said. He put out an arm for the man to catch hold of. To my surprise, he accepted Thorbjorn's help, letting the younger man guide him out of the hall and into the rain.

"Mormor? Did he really have the power to bring down a curse?" I asked, whispering, although Vali was surely unable to hear me after those heavy doors had slammed shut again.

"No," she said with a sad shake of her head. "He had no artifact, no focus of power, nothing. Only a lot of bad feelings that poisoned his heart. No one was ever in any danger."

"That's a relief, anyway," Valki said.

"And no families are owing a blood price long unpaid," Brigida reminded him. "That's no bad thing either."

But that, to me, was no cause for feelings of relief, either. Because that meant the problems still persisted. Something was making Esja sick more days than she was well, and no one was any closer to figuring out why that was.

And Kara, due to be married in less than a month, had no idea about her family history of fertility problems. But the first step towards solving that problem was at least an easy one, comparatively speaking.

I would simply not relent until her parents told her and Nilda the truth. I might not have Loke's natural skills with irritating people, but I could be annoying enough, in my own way.

If only all the problems facing me could be dealt with so handily.

CHAPTER TWENTY-THREE

IT WAS hours before the council meeting finally broke up, and my grandmother and I were free to go.

At least the rain had stopped. When we stepped outside, it was late afternoon. The sun was shining brightly, surprisingly hot for how low it was in the west. It was drying up the water droplets that clung to the plants in the gardens across from the hall.

The apple blossom smell was almost gone now, but a hint of it still lingered. Apple butter, perfect for waffles.

I was so hungry.

"I don't think you will find anything that Nilda missed when you go out to the wilds, but I agree it is a necessary trip," my grandmother said to me. It took me a moment to run back in my mind over the hours of droning council decisions to my declaration to make that journey.

"If I can get Loke to help me, it won't take much time," I said. I turned away from the garden to head back up the hill to my house in the village, and my grandmother walked along beside me. The end of her wooden staff kept pace beside her.

"You no longer need me to stand between you and the council," she said after a few moments of quiet walking.

"I wouldn't say that," I objected, but she was already shaking her head.

"I would. You are ready," she said firmly. "And I have things of my own to tend to."

"Like what?" I asked.

She gave me a sly look out of the corner of her eyes. "I have business in Runde."

"Opening the mead hall again?" I asked. I couldn't help looking back over my shoulder at the council hall, already out of sight behind us. She hadn't mentioned it in the meeting, and there had been plenty of opportunities. So many less important topics had been talked to death.

"No, not just yet," she assured me. "I have to rebuild my cabin first. I have to have a home in Runde before I can work that magic again."

"Spanning the two worlds is part of it?" I asked.

"Why do you think Loke's magic is so useful to draw from to maintain the mead hall? He's the very essence of spanning the worlds. But I can do it on my own again, once I have a home there," she said. We had reached my front gate, but my grandmother stayed in the middle of the road.

"Do you want me to walk with you to the forest path?" I asked.

"No, actually. But I would like you to walk with me to the meadow," she said.

"You're going down to Runde so soon?" I asked.

"It's time," she said. She smiled at me. She had nothing with her but the jacket on her back and the staff in her hands. And yet I knew she was ready. She had all she needed.

We walked together, through the empty village square and then east through the narrowest strip of village and then through the forest of beech trees to the meadow.

"You knew I went to see Halldis," I said at last.

"Yes," she said simply.

"You knew why?" I pressed.

She thought about that one for a few steps, then said, "when I knew you went to see her, I had a good guess as to why."

"She didn't tell me anything, really. But seeing her confirmed things in my mind, I guess," I said.

"She won't give up anything willingly," my grandmother said. "I wouldn't recommend going back to her until you know just what to ask, and just how to make her answer."

"But that's just a recommendation?" I asked.

I was joking, but she was quite serious when she said, "yes."

"Okay," I said, more gob struck than ever.

So many things were changing, so fast.

"Torfa's fire," I said suddenly. At first it was because that was the one thing that I thought had caused all this change. But at my grandmother's questioning look, I said, "your grandmother told me that each volva can visit it three times, and three times only. You've been there once?"

"Once," she agreed with a nod. "I'm not sure I would ever wish to go back there, myself. That fire had an energy… I don't think it was friendly to me."

"None of us felt comfortable there," I said with a shiver.

"Not even Loke?" she asked me.

"Loke wouldn't go near it more than he had to," I said. "Which was more than Mjolner would do, come to think of it."

"Some things are better not used, save in dire emergency," she said. "I think that fire is definitely one of those things."

"I used up my access to it in just a couple of days," I admitted with a sigh.

"You'll find other sources of power," my grandmother said with certainty.

We had reached the meadow, the grass so wet from the rain it was soaking through my pants. My grandmother stopped at the mouth of the cave with the staircase that led down to all the other caverns. Then she turned to me with a smile.

"I think you've spent enough time down here in the dark. I can walk alone from here," she said.

"Are you sure?" I asked.

"Quite. Stay out in the sun. Soak it in. You're looking quite pale," she said.

"Thanks," I said, touching my cheek. As if I could somehow feel my own paleness.

"I'll be back in town soon enough. So much wedding planning going on, and we all have jobs to do. You'll have tasks yourself, I'm sure, now that your time sitting by the fire is done."

"I'm definitely done with sitting in the dark," I admitted. "In fact, I think I'm ready for my next rune. If it wouldn't give Haraldr a heart attack for me to go to him before he summoned me for a lesson."

"I think he'd find it a very good sign, my dear," my grandmother said. Then she kissed me on the cheek and disappeared down into the dark.

I walked to the edge of the meadow, looking out over Lake Superior. The rain clouds were still out there, hovering low over the gray waters, but slanted beams of sunshine were out there too, breaking up the gloom in patches of sparkling reflections on the waves.

I watched until I could see my grandmother's figure moving down the path, picking her way down the waterfall-slicked rocks to the overgrown riverbank and then on to the mead hall itself. She didn't go inside, just skirted around it.

But I knew that would change, soon enough. Soon it would be back, glowing in all its magical glory. She only needed a home first.

I turned back towards the west, then walked alone, back to Vill-mark, back to my own home in the heart of that village.

The place where I finally felt like I well and truly belonged.

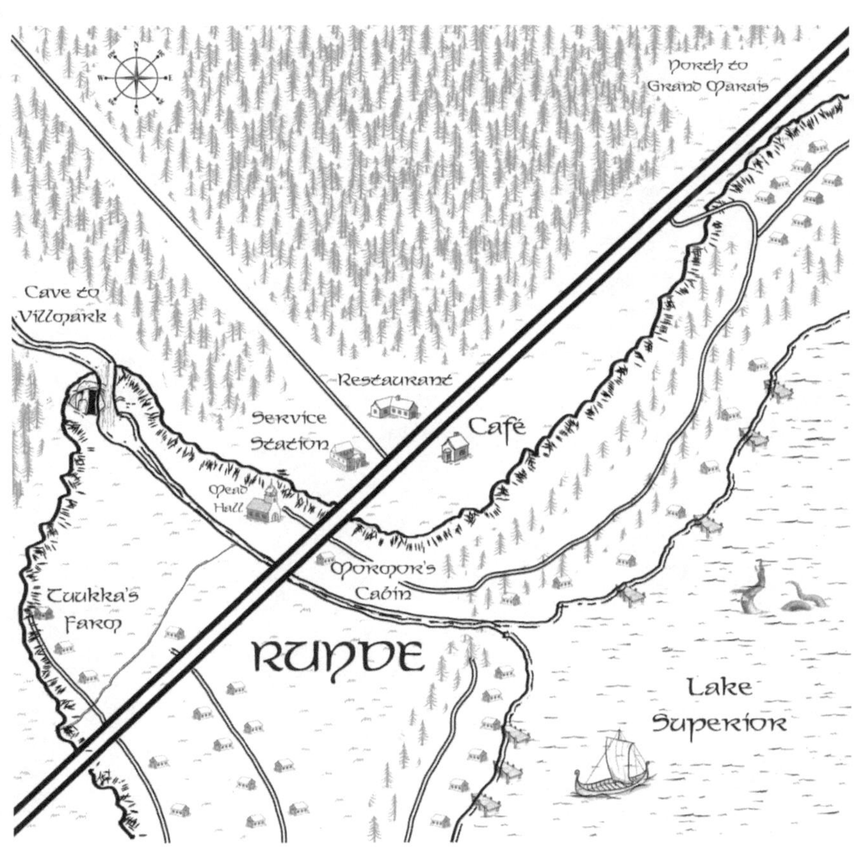

North to
Grand Marais
Cave to
Villmark
Restaurant
Service
Station
Café
Mead
Hall
Tuukka's
Farm
Mormor's
Cabin
RUNDE
Lake
Superior

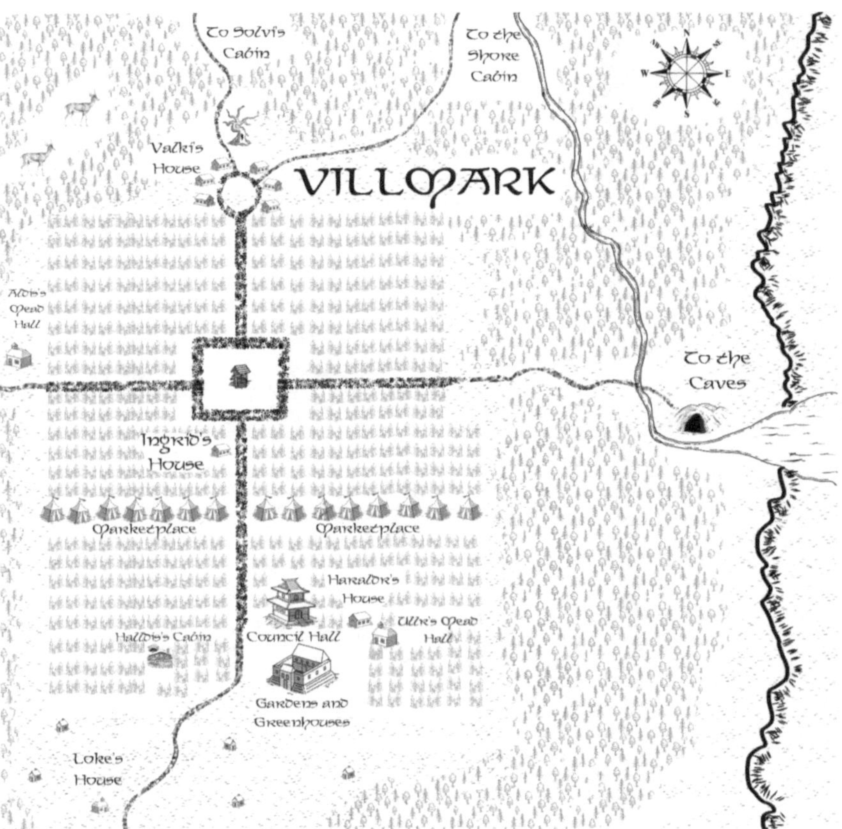

To Solvi's Cabin
To the Shore Cabin
Valki's House
VILLMARK
Aldis's Mead Hall
Ingrid's House
Marketplace
Marketplace
Haraldr's House
Ullr's Mead Hall
Halldis's Cabin
Council Hall
Gardens and Greenhouses
Loke's House
To the Caves
N
S
E
W
NE
NW
SE
SW

CHECK OUT BOOK TEN!

The Viking Witch will return in **Body Under the Café,** available now!

Ingrid Torfudottir lives in two worlds at once. The first, Runde, lies on the banks of Lake Superior, a town of northern Minnesotans who descend from Scandinavian immigrants, fishermen and farmers both. In that world she barely exists, just an unknown aspiring book illustrator who occasionally sells a little art at the local café.

The other, Villmark, lies hidden from the rest of the world by ancient, strong magic. The people of the village descend from colonists who fled their homeland in Norway centuries before. In that world she bears great responsibilities. As a volva, a Viking witch, the protection of her people always comes first in her life.

These two worlds overlap in just one place: her grandmother's mead hall. After sitting abandoned for months, Ingrid and her grandmother open it again to much celebration in both communities.

But then everything goes wrong. The illusions and protections remain despite their efforts at the end of the night. And Ingrid can't get back to Villmark.

Then someone dies, a murder. As if Ingrid didn't have enough on her plate.

Body Under the Café is book 10 in **The Viking Witch Mystery Series**!

THE WITCHES THREE
COZY MYSTERIES

In case you missed it, check out **Charm School**, the first book in the complete **Witches Three Cozy Mystery Series**!

Amanda Clarke thinks of herself as perfectly ordinary in every way. Just a small-town girl who serves breakfast all day in a little diner nestled next to the highway, nothing but dairy farms for miles around. She fits in there.

But then an old woman she never met dies, and Amanda was named in her will. Now Amanda packs a bag and heads to the big city, to Miss Zenobia Weekes' Charm School for Exceptional Young Ladies. And it's not in just any neighborhood. No, she finds herself on Summit Avenue in St. Paul, a street lined with gorgeous old houses, the former homes of lumber barons, railroad millionaires, even the writer F. Scott Fitzgerald. Why, Amanda can practically hear the jazz music still playing across the decades.

Scratch that. The music really, literally, still plays in the backyard of the charm school. Because the house stretches across time itself. Without a witch to protect this tear in the fabric of the world, anything can spill over. Like music.

Or like murder.

Charm School, the first book in the complete **Witches Three Cozy Mystery Series!**

THE WEAL & WOE BOOKSHOP WITCH MYSTERIES

In case you missed it, check out **The Teashop Terror,** the first book in the complete **Weal & Woe Bookshop Witch Mystery Series**!

No one knows more about every branch of magic than Tabitha Greene. She devoted years to studying the most esoteric texts, hunting down the most obscure source materials, and deciphering the most cryptic ancient scrolls. But her career in academia hits a dead end when no wizard will take her on as an apprentice.

Just because, despite being descended from two long and prestigious lines of witches, her attempts to actually perform any magic always fail. Often spectacularly.

But no more college means no more dorm life. And no magical skills means no real job skills, at least, not in the witchy world. And a life spent moving from school to school every few months was a life without real friendships. She finds herself alone with nowhere to go.

Then an uncle she barely remembers offers her a summer job, running his bookstore over the summer. The Weal and Woe Bookstore, located in a magical pocket world within a block of buildings just north of the old Mill District of Minneapolis, Minnesota.

Not exactly the pinnacle of all her hopes and dreams. But it's just for one summer, right?

Or so Tabitha tells herself. But unbeknownst to her, the Weal and Woe Bookstore is about to change her life.

The Teashop Terror, the first book in the complete **Weal & Woe Bookshop Witch Mystery Series**!

The Ritchie and Fitz Sci-Fi Murder Mysteries starts with **Murder on the Intergalactic Railway**.

For Murdina Ritchie, acceptance at the Oymyakon Foreign Service Academy means one last chance at her dream of becoming a diplomat for the Union of Free Worlds. For Shackleton Fitz IV, it represents his last chance not to fail out of military service entirely.

Strange that fate should throw them together now, among the last group of students admitted after the start of the semester. They had once shared the strongest of friendships. But that all ended a long time ago.

But when an insufferable but politically important woman turns up murdered, the two agree to put their differences aside and work together to solve the case.

Because the murderer might strike again. But more importantly, solving a murder would just have to impress the dour colonel who clearly thinks neither of them belong at his academy.

Murder on the Intergalactic Railway, the first book in **The Ritchie**

and Fitz Sci-Fi Murder Mysteries, available everywhere books are sold.

FREE EBOOK!

Like exclusive, free content?

If you'd like to receive "A Collection of Witchy Prequels", a free collection of short story prequels to the Witches Three Cozy Mystery and Viking Witch Mystery series, as well as other free stories throughout the year, go to my website CateMartin.com to subscribe to my newsletter! This eBook is exclusively for newsletter subscribers and will never be sold in stores. Check it out!

ABOUT THE AUTHOR

Cate Martin has written stories which have appeared in **Mystery, Crime and Mayhem** quarterly magazine as well as in the annual **Holiday Spectacular** Advent calendar of Christmas stories. She is also the author of three witch mystery series: **The Witches Three Cozy Mysteries**, and **The Viking Witch Mysteries** and **The Weal and Woe Bookshop Witch Mysteries**. She currently lives in Minneapolis, Minnesota. You can learn more about her work at CateMartin.com.

ALSO BY CATE MARTIN

The Witches Three Cozy Mystery Series

Charm School

Work Like a Charm

Third Time is a Charm

Old World Charm

Charm his Pants Off

Charm Offensive

The Witches Three Cozy Mysteries Books 1-3

The Witches Three Cozy Mysteries Books 4-6

The Viking Witch Mystery Series

Body at the Crossroads

Death Under the Bridge

Murder on the Lake

Killing in the Village Commons

Bloodshed in the Forest

Corpse in the Mead Hall

Slaying on the Lake Shore

Bones by the Forest Road

Sacrifice Behind the Falls

Body Under the Café

Assassination in the Glade

Bewitchment After the Storm

Predator in the Lanes

Threat From the North

Snare in the Blind Alley

Ashes Beneath the Tree (available July 14, 2026 direct from me or August 11, 2026 in stores everywhere)

The Viking Witch Mysteries Books 1-3

The Viking Witch Mysteries Books 4-6

The Viking Witch Mysteries Books 7-9

The Weal & Woe Bookshop Witch Mystery Series

The Teashop Terror

The Salon & Spa Scandal

The Bookseller Blunder

The Entrepreneur Enigma

The Novelty Shop Nightmare

The Courtyard Conundrum

Short Story Collections

Bubbly, Bicycles and Brides

The Dorothy Lundegaard Mysteries

Fruitcake, Festivities and Firelight